The Best of
W.W. Jacobs

W.W. Jacobs

The Best of W.W. Jacobs
containing

The White Cat
The Changing Numbers
Husbandry
A Golden Venture
Captain Rogers
Deserted

Contents

THE BEST OF
W.W. JACOBS

BY

W.W. Jacobs

THE WHITE CAT

THE WHITE CAT

The traveller stood looking from the tap-room window of the *Cauliflower* at the falling rain. The village street below was empty, and everything was quiet with the exception of the garrulous old man smoking with much enjoyment on the settle behind him.

"It'll do a power o' good," said the ancient, craning his neck round the edge of the settle and turning a bleared eye on the window. "I ain't like some folk; I never did mind a drop o' rain."

The traveller grunted and, returning to the settle opposite the old man, fell to lazily stroking a cat which had strolled in attracted by the warmth of the small fire which smouldered in the grate.

"He's a good mouser," said the old man, "but I expect that Smith the landlord would sell 'im to anybody for arf a crown; but we 'ad a cat in Claybury once that you couldn't ha' bought for a hundred golden sovereigns."

The traveller continued to caress the cat.

"A white cat, with one yaller eye and one blue one," continued the old man. "It sounds queer, but it's as true as I sit 'ere wishing that I 'ad another mug o' ale as good as the last you gave me."

The traveller, with a start that upset the cat's nerves, finished his own mug, and then ordered both to be refilled. He stirred the fire into a blaze, and, lighting his pipe and putting one foot on to the hob, prepared to listen.

It used to belong to old man Clark, young Joe Clark's uncle, said the ancient, smacking his lips delicately over the ale and extending a tremulous claw to the tobacco-pouch pushed towards him; and he was never tired of showing it off to people. He used to call it 'is blue-eyed darling, and the fuss 'e made o' that cat was sinful.

Young Joe Clark couldn't bear it, but being down in 'is uncle's will for five cottages and a bit o' land bringing in about forty pounds a year, he 'ad to 'ide his feelings and pretend as he loved it. He used to take it little drops o' cream and tit-bits o' meat, and old Clark was so pleased that 'e promised 'im that he should 'ave the cat along with all the other property when 'e was dead.

Young Joe said he couldn't thank 'im enough, and the old man, who 'ad been ailing a long time, made 'im come up every day to teach 'im 'ow to take care of it arter he was gone. He taught Joe 'ow to cook its meat and then chop it up fine; 'ow it liked a clean saucer every time for its milk; and 'ow he wasn't to make a noise when it was asleep.

"Take care your children don't worry it, Joe," he ses one day, very sharp. "One o' your boys was pulling its tail this morning, and I want you to clump his 'ead for 'im."

"Which one was it?" ses Joe.

"The slobbery-nosed one," ses old Clark.

"I'll give 'im a clout as soon as I get 'ome," ses Joe, who was very fond of 'is children.

"Go and fetch 'im and do it 'ere," ses the old man; "that'll teach 'im to love animals."

Joe went off 'ome to fetch the boy, and arter his mother 'ad washed his face, and wiped his nose, an' put a clean pinneyfore on 'im, he took 'im to 'is uncle's and clouted his 'ead for 'im. Arter that Joe and 'is wife 'ad words all night long, and next morning old Clark, coming in from the garden, was just in time to see 'im kick the cat right acrost the kitchen.

He could 'ardly speak for a minute, and when 'e could Joe see plain wot a fool he'd been. Fust of all 'e called Joe every name he could think of-- which took 'im a long time--and then he ordered 'im out of 'is house.

"You shall 'ave my money wen your betters have done with it," he ses, "and not afore. That's all you've done for yourself."

Joe Clark didn't know wot he meant at the time, but when old Clark died three months arterwards 'e found out. His uncle 'ad made a new will and left everything to old George Barstow for as long as the cat lived, providing that he took care of it. When the cat was dead the property was to go to Joe.

The cat was only two years old at the time, and George Barstow, who was arf crazy with joy, said it shouldn't be 'is fault if it didn't live another twenty years.

The funny thing was the quiet way Joe Clark took it. He didn't seem to be at all cut up about it, and when Henery Walker said it was a shame, 'e said he didn't mind, and that George Barstow was a old man, and he was quite welcome to 'ave the property as long as the cat lived.

"It must come to me by the time I'm an old man," he ses, "ard that's all I care about."

Henery Walker went off, and as 'e passed the cottage where old Clark used to live, and which George Barstow 'ad moved into, 'e spoke to the old man over the palings and told 'im wot Joe Clark 'ad said. George Barstow only grunted and went on stooping and prying over 'is front garden.

"Bin and lost something?" ses Henery Walker, watching 'im.

"No; I'm finding," ses George Barstow, very fierce, and picking up something. "That's the fifth bit o' powdered liver I've found in my garden this morning."

Henery Walker went off whistling, and the opinion he'd 'ad o' Joe Clark began to improve. He spoke to Joe about it that arternoon, and Joe said that if 'e ever accused 'im o' such a thing again he'd knock 'is 'ead off. He said that he 'oped the cat 'ud live to be a hundred, and that 'e'd no more think of giving it poisoned meat than Henery Walker would of paying for 'is drink so long as 'e could get anybody else to do it for 'im.

They 'ad bets up at this 'ere *Cauliflower* public-'ouse that evening as to 'ow long that cat 'ud live. Nobody gave it more than a month, and Bill Chambers sat and thought o' so many ways o' killing it on the sly that it was wunnerful to hear 'im.

George Barstow took fright when he 'eard of them, and the care 'e took o' that cat was wunnerful to behold. Arf its time it was shut up in the back bedroom, and the other arf George Barstow was fussing arter it till that cat got to hate 'im like pison. Instead o' giving up work as he'd thought to do, 'e told Henery Walker that 'e'd never worked so 'ard in his life.

"Wot about fresh air and exercise for it?" ses Henery.

"Wot about Joe Clark?" ses George Bar-stow. "I'm tied 'and and foot. I dursent leave the house for a moment. I ain't been to the *Cauliflower* since I've 'ad it, and three times I got out o' bed last night to see if it was safe."

"Mark my words," ses Henery Walker; "if that cat don't 'ave exercise, you'll lose it.

"I shall lose it if it does 'ave exercise," ses George Barstow, "that I know."

He sat down thinking arter Henery Walker 'ad gone, and then he 'ad a little collar and chain made for it, and took it out for a walk. Pretty nearly every dog in Claybury went with 'em, and the cat was in such a state o' mind afore they got 'ome he couldn't do anything with it. It 'ad a fit as soon as they got indoors, and George Barstow, who 'ad read about children's fits in the almanac, gave it a warm bath. It brought it round immediate, and then it began to tear round the room and up and downstairs till George Barstow was afraid to go near it.

It was so bad that evening, sneezing, that George Barstow sent for Bill Chambers, who'd got a good name for doctoring animals, and asked 'im to give it something. Bill said he'd got some powders at 'ome that would cure it at once, and he went and fetched 'em and mixed one up with a bit o' butter.

"That's the way to give a cat medicine," he ses; "smear it with the butter and then it'll lick it off, powder and all."

He was just going to rub it on the cat when George Barstow caught 'old of 'is arm and stopped 'im.

"How do I know it ain't pison?" he ses. "You're a friend o' Joe Clark's, and for all I know he may ha' paid you to pison it."

"I wouldn't do such a thing," ses Bill. "You ought to know me better than that."

"All right," ses George Barstow; "you eat it then, and I'll give you two shillings in stead o' one. You can easy mix some more."

"Not me," ses Bill Chambers, making a face.

"Well, three shillings, then," ses George Barstow, getting more and more suspicious like; "four shillings--five shillings."

Bill Chambers shook his 'ead, and George Barstow, more and more certain that he 'ad caught 'im trying to kill 'is cat and that 'e wouldn't eat the stuff, rose 'im up to ten shillings.

Bill looked at the butter and then 'e looked at the ten shillings on the table, and at last he shut 'is eyes and gulped it down and put the money in 'is pocket.

"You see, I 'ave to be careful, Bill," ses George Barstow, rather upset.

He 'ad a little collar and chain made for it, and took it out for a walk.

Bill Chambers didn't answer 'im. He sat there as white as a sheet, and making such extraordinary faces that George was arf afraid of 'im.

"Anything wrong, Bill?" he ses at last.

Bill sat staring at 'im, and then all of a sudden he clapped 'is 'andkerchief to 'is mouth and, getting up from his chair, opened the door and rushed out. George Barstow thought at fust that he 'ad eaten pison for the sake o' the ten shillings, but when 'e remembered that Bill Chambers 'ad got the most delikit stummick in Clay-bury he altered 'is mind.

The cat was better next morning, but George Barstow had 'ad such a fright about it 'e wouldn't let it go out of 'is sight, and Joe Clark began to think that 'e would 'ave to wait longer for that property than 'e had thought, arter all. To 'ear 'im talk anybody'd ha' thought that 'e loved that cat. We didn't pay much attention to it up at the *Cauliflower* 'ere, except maybe to wink at 'im--a thing he couldn't a bear--but at 'ome, o' course, his young 'uns thought as everything he said was Gospel; and one day, coming 'ome from work, as he was passing George Barstow's he was paid out for his deceitfulness.

"I've wronged you, Joe Clark," ses George Barstow, coming to the door, "and I'm sorry for it."

"Oh!" ses Joe, staring.

"Give that to your little Jimmy," ses George Barstow, giving 'im a shilling. "I've give 'im one, but I thought arterwards it wasn't enough."

"What for?" ses Joe, staring at 'im agin.

"For bringing my cat 'ome," ses George Barstow. "'Ow it got out I can't think, but I lost it for three hours, and I'd about given it up when your little Jimmy brought it to me in 'is arms. He's a fine little chap and 'e does you credit."

Joe Clark tried to speak, but he couldn't get a word out, and Henery Walker, wot 'ad just come up and 'eard wot passed, took hold of 'is arm and helped 'im home. He walked like a man in a dream, but arf-way he stopped and cut a stick from the hedge to take 'ome to little Jimmy. He said the boy 'ad been asking him for a stick for some time, but up till then 'e'd always forgotten it.

At the end o' the fust year that cat was still alive, to everybody's surprise; but George Barstow took such care of it 'e never let it out of 'is sight. Every time 'e went out he took it with 'im in a hamper, and, to prevent its being pisoned, he paid Isaac

Sawyer, who 'ad the biggest family in Claybury, sixpence a week to let one of 'is boys taste its milk before it had it.

The second year it was ill twice, but the horse-doctor that George Barstow got for it said that it was as 'ard as nails, and with care it might live to be twenty. He said that it wanted more fresh air and exercise; but when he 'eard 'ow George Barstow come by it he said that p'r'aps it would live longer indoors arter all.

At last one day, when George Barstow 'ad been living on the fat o' the land for nearly three years, that cat got out agin. George 'ad raised the front-room winder two or three inches to throw something outside, and, afore he knew wot was 'appening, the cat was out-side and going up the road about twenty miles an hour.

George Barstow went arter it, but he might as well ha' tried to catch the wind. The cat was arf wild with joy at getting out agin, and he couldn't get within arf a mile of it.

He stayed out all day without food or drink, follering it about until it came on dark, and then, o' course, he lost sight of it, and, hoping against 'ope that it would come home for its food, he went 'ome and waited for it. He sat up all night dozing in a chair in the front room with the door left open, but it was all no use; and arter thinking for a long time wot was best to do, he went out and told some o' the folks it was lost and offered a reward of five pounds for it.

You never saw such a hunt then in all your life. Nearly every man, woman, and child in Claybury left their work or school and went to try and earn that five pounds. By the arternoon George Barstow made it ten pounds provided the cat was brought 'ome safe and sound, and people as was too old to walk stood at their cottage doors to snap it up as it came by.

Joe Clark was hunting for it 'igh and low, and so was 'is wife and the boys. In fact, I b'lieve that everybody in Claybury excepting the parson and Bob Pretty was trying to get that ten pounds.

O' course, we could understand the parson--'is pride wouldn't let 'im; but a low, poaching, thieving rascal like Bob Pretty turning up 'is nose at ten pounds was more than we could make out. Even on the second day, when George Barstow made it ten pounds down and a shilling a week for a year besides, he didn't offer to stir; all he did was to try and make fun o' them as was looking for it.

"Have you looked everywhere you can think of for it, Bill?" he ses to Bill Chambers. "Yes, I 'ave," ses Bill.

"Well, then, you want to look everywhere else," ses Bob Pretty. "I know where I should look if I wanted to find it."

"Why don't you find it, then?" ses Bill.

"'Cos I don't want to make mischief," ses Bob Pretty. "I don't want to be un-neighbourly to Joe Clark by interfering at all."

"Not for all that money?" ses Bill.

"Not for fifty pounds," ses Bob Pretty; "you ought to know me better than that, Bill Chambers."

"It's my belief that you know more about where that cat is than you ought to," ses Joe Gubbins.

"You go on looking for it, Joe," ses Bob Pretty, grinning; "it's good exercise for you, and you've only lost two days' work."

"I'll give you arf a crown if you let me search your 'ouse, Bob," ses Bill Chambers, looking at 'im very 'ard.

"I couldn't do it at the price, Bill," ses Bob Pretty, shaking his 'ead. "I'm a pore man, but I'm very partikler who I 'ave come into my 'ouse."

O' course, everybody left off looking at once when they heard about Bob-- not that they believed that he'd be such a fool as to keep the cat in his 'ouse; and that evening, as soon as it was dark, Joe Clark went round to see 'im.

"Don't tell me as that cat's found, Joe," ses Bob Pretty, as Joe opened the door.

"Not as I've 'eard of," said Joe, stepping inside. "I wanted to speak to you about it; the sooner it's found the better I shall be pleased."

"It does you credit, Joe Clark," ses Bob Pretty.

"It's my belief that it's dead," ses Joe, looking at 'im very 'ard; "but I want to make sure afore taking over the property."

Bob Pretty looked at 'im and then he gave a little cough. "Oh, you want it to be found dead," he ses. "Now, I wonder whether that cat's worth most dead or alive?"

Joe Clark coughed then. "Dead, I should think," he ses at last. "George Barstow's just 'ad bills printed offering fifteen pounds for it," ses Bob Pretty.

"I'll give that or more when I come into the property," ses Joe Clark.

"There's nothing like ready-money, though, is there?" ses Bob.

"I'll promise it to you in writing, Bob," ses Joe, trembling.

"There's some things that don't look well in writing, Joe," says Bob Pretty, considering; "besides, why should you promise it to me?"

"O' course, I meant if you found it," ses Joe.

"Well, I'll do my best, Joe," ses Bob Pretty; "and none of us can do no more than that, can they?"

They sat talking and argufying over it for over an hour, and twice Bob Pretty got up and said 'e was going to see whether George Barstow wouldn't offer more. By the time they parted they was as thick as thieves, and next morning Bob Pretty was wearing Joe Clark's watch and chain, and Mrs. Pretty was up at Joe's 'ouse to see whether there was any of 'is furniture as she 'ad a fancy for.

She didn't seem to be able to make up 'er mind at fust between a chest o' drawers that 'ad belonged to Joe's mother and a grand-father clock. She walked from one to the other for about ten minutes, and then Bob, who 'ad come in to 'elp her, told 'er to 'ave both.

"You're quite welcome," he ses; "ain't she, Joe?"

Joe Clark said "Yes," and arter he 'ad helped them carry 'em 'ome the Prettys went back and took the best bedstead to pieces, cos Bob said as it was easier to carry that way. Mrs. Clark 'ad to go and sit down at the bottom o' the garden with the neck of 'er dress undone to give herself air, but when she saw the little Prettys each walking 'ome with one of 'er best chairs on their 'eads she got and walked up and down like a mad thing.

"I'm sure I don't know where we are to put it all," ses Bob Pretty to Joe Gubbins, wot was looking on with other folks, "but Joe Clark is that generous he won't 'ear of our leaving anything."

"Has 'e gorn mad?" ses Bill Chambers, staring at 'im.

"Not as I knows on," ses Bob Pretty. "It's 'is good-'artedness, that's all. He feels sure that that cat's dead, and that he'll 'ave George Barstow's cottage and furniture. I told 'im he'd better wait till he'd made sure, but 'e wouldn't."

Before they'd finished the Prettys 'ad picked that 'ouse as clean as a bone, and Joe Clark 'ad to go and get clean straw for his wife and children to sleep on; not that Mrs. Clark 'ad any sleep that night, nor Joe neither.

Henery Walker was the fust to see what it really meant, and he went rushing off as fast as 'e could run to tell George Barstow. George couldn't believe 'im at fust, but when 'e did he swore that if a 'air of that cat's head was harmed 'e'd 'ave the law o' Bob Pretty, and arter Henery Walker 'ad gone 'e walked round to tell 'im so.

"You're not yourself, George Barstow, else you wouldn't try and take away my character like that," ses Bob Pretty.

"Wot did Joe Clark give you all them things for?" ses George, pointing to the furniture.

"Took a fancy to me, I s'pose," ses Bob. "People do sometimes. There's something about me at times that makes 'em like me."

"He gave 'em to you to kill my cat," ses George Barstow. "It's plain enough for any-body to see."

Bob Pretty smiled. "I expect it'll turn up safe and sound one o' these days," he ses, "and then you'll come round and beg my pardon. P'r'aps--"

"P'r'aps wot?" ses George Barstow, arter waiting a bit.

"P'r'aps somebody 'as got it and is keeping it till you've drawed the fifteen pounds out o' the bank," ses Bob, looking at 'im very hard.

"I've taken it out o' the bank," ses George, starting; "if that cat's alive, Bob, and you've got it, there's the fifteen pounds the moment you 'and it over."

"Wot d'ye mean--me got it?" ses Bob Pretty. "You be careful o' my character."

"I mean if you know where it is," ses George Barstow trembling all over.

"I don't say I couldn't find it, if that's wot you mean," ses Bob. "I can gin'rally find things when I want to."

"You find me that cat, alive and well, and the money's yours, Bob," ses George, 'ardly able to speak, now that 'e fancied the cat was still alive.

Bob Pretty shook his 'ead. "No; that won't do," he ses. "S'pose I did 'ave the luck to find that pore animal, you'd say I'd had it all the time and refuse to pay."

"I swear I wouldn't, Bob," ses George Barstow, jumping up.

"Best thing you can do if you want me to try and find that cat," says Bob Pretty, "is to give me the fifteen pounds now, and I'll go and look for it at once. I can't trust you, George Barstow."

"And I can't trust you," ses George Barstow.

"Very good," ses Bob, getting up; "there's no 'arm done. P'r'aps Joe Clark 'll find the cat is dead and p'r'aps you'll find it's alive. It's all one to me."

George Barstow walked off 'ome, but he was in such a state o' mind 'e didn't know wot to do. Bob Pretty turning up 'is nose at fifteen pounds like that made 'im think that Joe Clark 'ad promised to pay 'im more if the cat was dead; and at last, arter worrying about it for a couple o' hours, 'e came up to this 'ere *Cauliflower* and offered Bob the fifteen pounds.

"Wot's this for?" ses Bob.

"For finding my cat," ses George.

"Look here," ses Bob, handing it back, "I've 'ad enough o' your insults; I don't know where your cat is."

"I mean for trying to find it, Bob," ses George Barstow.

"Oh, well, I don't mind that," ses Bob, taking it. "I'm a 'ard-working man, and I've got to be paid for my time; it's on'y fair to my wife and children. I'll start now."

He finished up 'is beer, and while the other chaps was telling George Barstow wot a fool he was Joe Clark slipped out arter Bob Pretty and began to call 'im all the names he could think of.

"Don't you worry," ses Bob; "the cat ain't found yet."

"Is it dead?" ses Joe Clark, 'ardly able to speak.

"'Ow should I know?" ses Bob; "that's wot I've got to try and find out. That's wot you gave me your furniture for, and wot George Barstow gave me the fifteen pounds for, ain't it? Now, don't you stop me now, 'cos I'm goin' to begin looking."

He started looking there and then, and for the next two or three days George Barstow and Joe Clark see 'im walking up and down with his 'ands in 'is pockets looking over garden fences and calling "Puss." He asked everybody 'e see whether they 'ad seen a white cat with one blue eye and one yaller one, and every time 'e came into the *Cauliflower* he put his 'ead over the bar and called "Puss," 'cos, as 'e said, it was as likely to be there as anywhere else.

It was about a week after the cat 'ad disappeared that George Barstow was standing at 'is door talking to Joe Clark, who was saying the cat must be dead and 'e wanted 'is property, when he sees a man coming up the road carrying a basket stop and speak to Bill Chambers. Just as 'e got near them an awful "miaow" come from the basket and George Barstow and Joe Clark started as if they'd been shot.

"He's found it?" shouts Bill Chambers, pointing to the man.

"It's been living with me over at Ling for a week pretty nearly," ses the man. "I tried to drive it away several times, not knowing that there was fifteen pounds offered for it."

George Barstow tried to take 'old of the basket.

"I want that fifteen pounds fust," ses the man.

"That's on'y right and fair, George," ses Bob Pretty, who 'ad just come up. "You've got all the luck, mate. We've been hunting 'igh and low for that cat for a week."

Then George Barstow tried to explain to the man and call Bob Pretty names at the same time; but it was all no good. The man said it 'ad nothing to do with 'im wot he 'ad paid to Bob Pretty; and at last they fetched Policeman White over from Cudford, and George Barstow signed a paper to pay five shillings a week till the reward was paid.

George Barstow 'ad the cat for five years arter that, but he never let it get away agin. They got to like each other in time and died within a fortnight of each other, so that Joe Clark got 'is property arter all.

THE CHANGING NUMBERS

The tall clock in the corner of the small living-room had just struck eight as Mr. Samuel Gunnill came stealthily down the winding staircase and, opening the door at the foot, stepped with an appearance of great care and humility into the room. He noticed with some anxiety that his daughter Selina was apparently engrossed in her task of attending to the plants in the window, and that no preparations whatever had been made for breakfast.

"Mr. Samuel Gunnill came stealthily down the winding staircase."

Miss Gunnill's horticultural duties seemed interminable. She snipped off dead leaves with painstaking precision, and administered water with the jealous care of a druggist compounding a prescription; then, with her back still toward him, she gave vent to a sigh far too intense in its nature to have reference to such trivialities as plants. She repeated it twice, and at the second time Mr. Gunnill, almost without his knowledge, uttered a deprecatory cough.

His daughter turned with alarming swiftness and, holding herself very upright, favoured him with a glance in which indignation and surprise were very fairly mingled.

"That white one--that one at the end," said Mr. Gunnill, with an appearance of concentrated interest, "that's my fav'rite."

Miss Gunnill put her hands together, and a look of infinite long-suffering came upon her face, but she made no reply.

"Always has been," continued Mr. Gunnill, feverishly, "from a--from a cutting."

"Bailed out," said Miss Gunnill, in a deep and thrilling voice; "bailed out at one o'clock in the morning, brought home singing loud enough for half-a-dozen, and then talking about flowers!"

Mr. Gunnill coughed again.

"I was dreaming," pursued Miss Gunnill, plaintively, "sleeping peacefully, when I was awoke by a horrible noise."

"That couldn't ha' been me," protested her father. "I was only a bit cheerful. It was Benjamin Ely's birthday yesterday, and after we left the Lion they started singing, and I just hummed to keep 'em company. I wasn't singing, mind you, only humming--when up comes that interfering Cooper and takes me off."

Miss Gunnill shivered, and with her pretty cheek in her hand sat by the window the very picture of despondency. "Why didn't he take the others?" she inquired.

"Ah!" said Mr. Gunnill, with great emphasis, "that's what a lot more of us would like to know. P'r'aps if you'd been more polite to Mrs. Cooper, instead o' putting it about that she looked young enough to be his mother, it wouldn't have happened."

His daughter shook her head impatiently and, on Mr. Gunnill making an allusion to breakfast, expressed surprise that he had got the heart to eat any-thing. Mr. Gunnill pressing the point, however, she arose and began to set the table, the undue care with which she smoothed out the creases of the table-cloth, and the mathematical exactness with which she placed the various articles, all being so many extra smarts in his wound. When she finally placed on the table enough food for a dozen people he began to show signs of a little spirit.

"Ain't you going to have any?" he demanded, as Miss Gunnill resumed her seat by the window.

"Me?" said the girl, with a shudder. "Breakfast? The disgrace is breakfast enough for me. I couldn't eat a morsel; it would choke me."

Mr. Gunnill eyed her over the rim of his teacup. "I come down an hour ago," he said, casually, as he helped himself to some bacon.

Miss Gunnill started despite herself. "Oh!" she said, listlessly.

"And I see you making a very good breakfast all by yourself in the kitchen," continued her father, in a voice not free from the taint of triumph.

The discomfited Selina rose and stood regarding him; Mr. Gunnill, after a vain attempt to meet her gaze, busied himself with his meal.

"The idea of watching every mouthful I eat!" said Miss Gunnill, tragically; "the idea of complaining because I have some breakfast! I'd never have believed it of you, never! It's shameful! Fancy grudging your own daughter the food she eats!"

Mr. Gunnill eyed her in dismay. In his confusion he had overestimated the capacity of his mouth, and he now strove in vain to reply to this shameful perversion of his meaning. His daughter stood watching him with grief in one eye and calculation in the other, and, just as he had put himself into a position to exercise his rights of free speech, gave a pathetic sniff and walked out of the room.

She stayed indoors all day, but the necessity of establishing his innocence took Mr. Gunnill out a great deal. His neighbours, in the hope of further excitement, warmly pressed him to go to prison rather than pay a fine, and instanced the example of an officer in the Salvation Army, who, in very different circumstances, had elected to take that course. Mr. Gunnill assured them that only his known antipathy to the army, and the fear of being regarded as one of its followers, prevented him from doing so. He paid instead a fine of ten shillings, and after listening to a sermon, in which his silver hairs served as the text, was permitted to depart. His feeling against Police-constable Cooper increased with the passing of the days. The constable watched him with the air of a proprietor, and Mrs. Cooper's remark that "her husband had had his eye upon him for a long time, and that he had better be careful for the future," was faithfully retailed to him within half an hour of its utterance. Convivial friends counted his cups for him; teetotal friends more than hinted that Cooper was in the employ of his good angel.

Miss Gunnill's two principal admirers had an arduous task to perform. They had to attribute Mr. Gunnill's disaster to the vindictiveness of Cooper, and at the same time to agree with his daughter that it served him right. Between father and daughter they had a difficult time, Mr. Gunnill's sensitiveness having been much heightened by his troubles.

"Cooper ought not to have taken you," said Herbert Sims for the fiftieth time.

"He must ha' seen you like it dozens o' times before," said Ted Drill, who, in his determination not to be outdone by Mr. Sims, was not displaying his usual judgment. "Why didn't he take you then? That's what you ought to have asked the magistrate."

"I don't understand you," said Mr. Gunnill, with an air of cold dignity.

"Why," said Mr. Drill, "what I mean is--look at that night, for instance, when----"

He broke off suddenly, even his enthusiasm not being proof against the extraordinary contortions of visage in which Mr. Gunnill was indulging.

"When?" prompted Selina and Mr. Sims together. Mr. Gunnill, after first daring him with his eye, followed suit.

"That night at the Crown," said Mr. Drill, awkwardly. "You know; when you thought that Joe Baggs was the landlord. You tell 'em; you tell it best. I've roared over it."

"I don't know what you're driving at," said the harassed Mr. Gunnill, bitterly.

"H'm!" said Mr. Drill, with a weak laugh. "I've been mixing you up with somebody else."

Mr. Gunnill, obviously relieved, said that he ought to be more careful, and pointed out, with some feeling, that a lot of mischief was caused that way.

"Cooper wants a lesson, that's what he wants," said Mr. Sims, valiantly. "He'll

" The constable watched him with the air of a proprietor."

get his head broke one of these days."

Mr. Gunnill acquiesced. "I remember when I was on the *Peewit,*" he said, musingly, "one time when we were lying at Cardiff, there was a policeman there run one of our chaps in, and two nights afterward another of our chaps pushed the policeman down in the mud and ran off with his staff and his helmet."

Miss Gunnill's eyes glistened. "What happened?" she inquired.

"He had to leave the force," replied her father; "he couldn't stand the disgrace of it. The chap that pushed him over was quite a little chap, too. About the size of Herbert here."

Mr. Sims started.

"Very much like him in face, too," pursued Mr. Gunnill; "daring chap he was."

Miss Gunnill sighed. "I wish he lived in Little-stow," she said, slowly. "I'd give anything to take that horrid Mrs. Cooper down a bit. Cooper would be the laughing-stock of the town."

Messrs. Sims and Drill looked unhappy. It was hard to have to affect an attitude of indifference in the face of Miss Gunnill's lawless yearnings; to stand before her as respectable and law-abiding cravens. Her eyes, large and sorrowful; dwelt on them both.

"If I--I only get a chance at Cooper!" murmured Mr. Sims, vaguely.

To his surprise, Mr. Gunnill started up from his chair and, gripping his hand, shook it fervently. He looked round, and Selina was regarding him with a glance so tender that he lost his head completely. Before he had recovered he had pledged himself to lay the helmet and truncheon of the redoubtable Mr. Cooper at the feet of Miss Gunnill; exact date not specified.

"Of course, I shall have to wait my opportunity," he said, at last.

"You wait as long as you like, my boy," said the thoughtless Mr. Gunnill.

Mr. Sims thanked him.

"Wait till Cooper's an old man," urged Mr. Drill.

Miss Gunnill, secretly disappointed at the lack of boldness and devotion on the part of the latter gentleman, eyed his stalwart frame indignantly and accused him of trying to make Mr. Sims as timid as himself. She turned to the valiant Sims and made herself so agreeable to that daring blade that Mr. Drill, a prey to violent jealousy, bade the company a curt good-night and withdrew.

He stayed away for nearly a week, and then one evening as he approached the house, carrying a carpet-bag, he saw the door just opening to admit the fortunate Herbert. He quickened his pace and arrived just in time to follow him in. Mr. Sims, who bore under his arm a brown-paper parcel, seemed somewhat embarrassed at seeing him, and after a brief greeting walked into the room, and with a triumphant glance at Mr. Gunnill and Selina placed his burden on the table.

" He saw the door just opening to admit the fortunate Herbert."

"You--you ain't got it?" said Mr. Gunnill, leaning forward.

"How foolish of you to run such a risk!" said Selina.

"I brought it for Miss Gunnill," said the young man, simply. He unfastened the parcel, and to the astonishment of all present revealed a policeman's helmet and a short boxwood truncheon.

"You--you're a wonder," said the gloating Mr. Gunnill. "Look at it, Ted!"

Mr. Drill was looking at it; it may be doubted whether the head of Mr. Cooper itself could have caused him more astonishment. Then his eyes sought those of Mr. Sims, but that gentleman was gazing tenderly at the gratified but shocked Selina.

"How ever did you do it?" inquired Mr. Gunnill.

"Came behind him and threw him down," said Mr. Sims, nonchalantly. "He was that scared I believe I could have taken his boots as well if I'd wanted them."

Mr. Gunnill patted him on the back. "I fancy I can see him running bare-headed through the town calling for help," he said, smiling.

Mr. Sims shook his head. "Like as not it'll be kept quiet for the credit of the force," he said, slowly, "unless, of course, they discover who did it."

A slight shade fell on the good-humoured countenance of Mr. Gunnill, but it was chased away almost immediately by Sims reminding him of the chaff of Cooper's brother-constables.

"And you might take the others away," said Mr. Gunnill, brightening; "you might keep on doing it."

Mr. Sims said doubtfully that he might, but pointed out that Cooper would probably be on his guard for the future.

"Yes, you've done your share," said Miss Gunnill, with a half-glance at Mr. Drill, who was still gazing in a bewildered fashion at the trophies. "You can come into the kitchen and help me draw some beer if you like."

Mr. Sims followed her joyfully, and reaching down a jug for her watched her tenderly as she drew the beer. All women love valour, but Miss Gunnill, gazing sadly at the slight figure of Mr. Sims, could not help wishing that Mr. Drill possessed a little of his spirit.

She had just finished her task when a tremendous bumping noise was heard in the living-room, and the plates on the dresser were nearly shaken off their shelves.

"What's that?" she cried.

They ran to the room and stood aghast in the doorway at the spectacle of Mr. Gunnill, with his clenched fists held tightly by his side, bounding into the air with

" Mr. Sims watched her tenderly as she drew the beer."

all the grace of a trained acrobat, while Mr. Drill encouraged him from an easy-chair. Mr. Gunnill smiled broadly as he met their astonished gaze, and with a final bound kicked something along the floor and subsided into his seat panting.

Mr. Sims, suddenly enlightened, uttered a cry of dismay and, darting under the table, picked up what had once been a policeman's helmet. Then he snatched a partially consumed truncheon from the fire, and stood white and trembling before the astonished Mr. Gunnill.

"What's the matter?" inquired the latter. "You--you've spoilt 'em," gasped Mr. Sims. "What of it?" said Mr. Gunnill, staring.

"I was--going to take 'em away," stammered Mr. Sims.

"Well, they'll be easier to carry now," said Mr. Drill, simply.

Mr. Sims glanced at him sharply, and then, to the extreme astonishment of Mr. Gunnill, snatched up the relics and, wrapping them up in the paper, dashed out of the house. Mr. Gunnill turned a look of blank inquiry upon Mr. Drill.

"It wasn't Cooper's number on the helmet," said that gentleman.

"Eh?" shouted Mr. Gunnill.

"How do you know?" inquired Selina.

"I just happened to notice," replied Mr. Drill. He reached down as though to take up the carpet-bag which he had placed by the side of his chair, and then, apparently thinking better of it, leaned back in his seat and eyed Mr. Gunnill.

"Do you mean to tell me," said the latter, "that he's been and upset the wrong man?"

Mr. Drill shook his head. "That's the puzzle," he said, softly.

He smiled over at Miss Gunnill, but that young lady, who found him somewhat mysterious, looked away and frowned. Her father sat and exhausted conjecture, his final conclusion being that Mr. Sims had attacked the first policeman that had come in his way and was now suffering the agonies of remorse.

He raised his head sharply at the sound of hurried footsteps outside. There was a smart rap at the street door, then the handle was turned, and the next moment, to the dismay of all present, the red and angry face of one of Mr. Cooper's brother-constables was thrust into the room.

Mr. Gunnill gazed at it in helpless fascination. The body of the constable garbed in plain clothes followed the face and, standing before him in a menacing fashion, held out a broken helmet and staff.

"Have you seen these afore?" he inquired, in a terrible voice.

"No," said Mr. Gunnill, with an attempt at surprise. "What are they?"

"I'll tell you what they are," said Police-constable Jenkins, ferociously; "they're my helmet and truncheon. You've been spoiling His Majesty's property, and you'll be locked up."

"Yours?" said the astonished Mr. Gunnill.

"I lent 'em to young Sims, just for a joke," said the constable. "I felt all along I was doing a silly thing."

"It's no joke," said Mr. Gunnill, severely. "I'll tell young Herbert what I think of him trying to deceive me like that."

"Never mind about deceiving," interrupted the constable. "What are you going to do about it?"

"What are you?" inquired Mr. Gunnill, hardily. "It seems to me it's between you and him; you'll very likely be dismissed from the force, and all through trying to deceive. I wash my hands of it."

"You'd no business to lend it," said Drill, interrupting the constable's indignant retort; "especially for Sims to pretend that he had stolen it from Cooper. It's a roundabout sort of thing, but you can't tell of Mr. Gunnill without getting into trouble yourself."

"I shall have to put up with that," said the constable, desperately; "it's got to be explained. It's my day-helmet, too, and the night one's as shabby as can be. Twenty years in the force and never a mark against my name till now."

"If you'd only keep quiet a bit instead of talking so much," said Mr. Drill, who had been doing some hard thinking, "I might be able to help you, p'r'aps."

"How?" inquired the constable.

"Help him if you can, Ted," said Mr. Gunnill, eagerly; "we ought all to help others when we get a chance."

Mr. Drill sat bolt upright and looked very wise.

He took the smashed helmet from the table and examined it carefully. It was broken in at least half-a-dozen places, and he laboured in vain to push it into shape. He might as well have tried to make a silk hat out of a concertina. The only thing that had escaped injury was the metal plate with the number.

"Why don't you mend it?" he inquired, at last.

"Mend it?" shouted the incensed Mr. Jenkins. "Why don't you?"

"I think I could," said Mr. Drill, slowly; "give me half an hour in the kitchen and I'll try."

"Have as long as you like," said Mr. Gunnill.

"And I shall want some glue, and Miss Gunnill, and some tin-tacks," said

Drill.

"What do you want me for?" inquired Selina.

"To hold the things for me," replied Mr. Drill.

Miss Gunnill tossed her head, but after a little demur consented; and Drill, ignoring the impatience of the constable, picked up his bag and led the way into the kitchen. Messrs. Gunnill and Jenkins, left behind in the living-room, sought for some neutral topic of discourse, but in vain; conversation would revolve round hard labour and lost pensions. From the kitchen came sounds of hammering, then a loud "Ooh!" from Miss Gunnill, followed by a burst of laughter and a clapping of hands. Mr. Jenkins shifted in his seat and exchanged glances with Mr. Gunnill.

[Illustration: "From the kitchen came sounds of hammering."]

"He's a clever fellow," said that gentleman, hopefully. "You should hear him imitate a canary; life-like it is."

Mr. Jenkins was about to make a hasty and obvious rejoinder, when the kitchen door opened and Selina emerged, followed by Drill. The snarl which the constable had prepared died away in a murmur of astonishment as he took the helmet. It looked as good as ever.

He turned it over and over in amaze, and looked in vain for any signs of the disastrous cracks. It was stiff and upright. He looked at the number: it was his own. His eyes round with astonishment he tried it on, and then his face relaxed.

"It don't fit as well as it did," he said.

"Well, upon my word, some people are never satisfied," said the indignant Drill. "There isn't another man in England could have done it better."

"I'm not grumbling," said the constable, hastily; "it's a wonderful piece o' work. Wonderful! I can't even see where it was broke. How on earth did you do it?"

Drill shook his head. "It's a secret process," he said, slowly. "I might want to go into the hat trade some day, and I'm not going to give things away."

"Quite right," said Mr. Jenkins. "Still--well, it's a marvel, that's what it is; a fair marvel. If you take my advice you'll go in the hat trade to-morrow, my lad."

"I'm not surprised," said Mr. Gunnill, whose face as he spoke was a map of astonishment. "Not a bit. I've seen him do more surprising things than that. Have a go at the staff now, Teddy."

"I'll see about it," said Mr. Drill, modestly. "I can't do impossibilities. You

" From the kitchen came sounds of hammering. "

leave it here, Mr. Jenkins, and we'll talk about it later on."

Mr. Jenkins, still marvelling over his helmet, assented, and, after another reference to the possibilities in the hat trade to a man with a born gift for repairs, wrapped his property in a piece of newspaper and departed, whistling.

"Ted," said Mr. Gunnill, impressively, as he sank into his chair with a sigh of relief. "How you done it I don't know. It's a surprise even to me."

"He is very clever," said Selina, with a kind smile

Mr. Drill turned pale, and then, somewhat emboldened by praise from such a quarter, dropped into a chair by her side and began to talk in low tones. The grateful Mr. Gunnill, more relieved than he cared to confess, thoughtfully closed his eyes.

"I didn't think all along that you'd let Herbert outdo you," said Selina.

"I want to outdo him," said Mr. Drill, in a voice of much meaning.

Miss Gunnill cast down her eyes and Mr. Drill had just plucked up sufficient courage to take her hand when footsteps stopped at the house, the handle of the door was turned, and, for the second time that evening, the inflamed visage of Mr. Jenkins confronted the company.

"Don't tell me it's a failure," said Mr. Gunnill, starting from his chair. "You must have been handling it roughly. It was as good as new when you took it away."

Mr. Jenkins waved him away and fixed his eyes upon Drill.

"You think you're mighty clever, I dare say," he said, grimly; "but I can put two and two together. I've just heard of it."

"Heard of two and two?" said Drill, looking puzzled.

"I don't want any of your nonsense," said Mr. Jenkins. "I'm not on duty now, but I warn you not to say anything that may be used against you."

"I never do," said Mr. Drill, piously.

"Somebody threw a handful o' flour in poor Cooper's face a couple of hours ago," said Mr. Jenkins, watching him closely, "and while he was getting it out of his eyes they upset him and made off with his helmet and truncheon. I just met Brown and he says Cooper's been going on like a madman."

"By Jove! it's a good job I mended your helmet for you," said Mr. Drill, "or else they might have suspected you."

Mr. Jenkins stared at him. "I know who did do it," he said, significantly.

"Herbert Sims?" guessed Mr. Drill, in a stage whisper.

"You'll be one o' the first to know," said Mr. Jenkins, darkly; "he'll be arrested to-morrow. Fancy the impudence of it! It's shocking."

Mr. Drill whistled. "Nell, don't let that little affair o' yours with Sims be known," he said, quietly. "Have that kept quiet--if you can."

Mr. Jenkins started as though he had been stung. In the joy of a case he had overlooked one or two things. He turned and regarded the young man wistfully.

"Don't call on me as a witness, that's all," continued Mr. Drill. "I never was a mischief-maker, and I shouldn't like to have to tell how you lent your helmet to Sims so that he could pretend he had knocked Cooper down and taken it from him."

[: "Don't call on me as a witness, that's all," continued Mr. Drill.]

"Wouldn't look at all well," said Mr. Gunnill, nodding his head sagely.

Mr. Jenkins breathed hard and looked from one to the other. It was plain that it was no good reminding them that he had not had a case for five years.

"When I say that I know who did it," he said, slowly, "I mean that I have my suspicions."

"Don't call on me as a witness, that's all,' continued Mr. Drill."

"Ah," said Mr. Drill, "that's a very different thing."

"Nothing like the same," said Mr. Gunnill, pouring the constable a glass of ale.

Mr. Jenkins drank it and smacked his lips feebly.

"Sims needn't know anything about that helmet being repaired," he said at last.

"Certainly not," said everybody.

Mr. Jenkins sighed and turned to Drill.

"It's no good spoiling the ship for a ha'porth o' tar," he said, with a faint suspicion of a wink. "No," said Drill, looking puzzled.

"Anything that's worth doing at all is worth doing well," continued the constable, "and while I'm drinking another glass with Mr. Gunnill here, suppose you go into the kitchen with that useful bag o' yours and finish repairing my truncheon?"

BOOK HUSBANDRY

Dealing with a man, said the night-watchman, thoughtfully, is as easy as a teetotaller walking along a nice wide pavement; dealing with a woman is like the same teetotaller, arter four or five whiskies, trying to get up a step that ain't there. If a man can't get 'is own way he eases 'is mind with a little nasty language, and then forgets all about it; if a woman can't get 'er own way she flies into a temper and reminds you of something you oughtn't to ha' done ten years ago. Wot a woman would do whose 'usband had never done anything wrong I can't think.

I remember a young feller telling me about a row he 'ad with 'is wife once. He 'adn't been married long and he talked as if the way she carried on was unusual. Fust of all, he said, she spoke to 'im in a cooing sort o' voice and pulled his moustache, then when he wouldn't give way she worked herself up into a temper and said things about 'is sister. Arter which she went out o' the room and banged the door so hard it blew down a vase off the fireplace. Four times she came back to tell 'im other things she 'ad thought of, and then she got so upset she 'ad to go up to bed and lay down instead of getting his tea. When that didn't do no good she refused her food, and when 'e took her up toast and tea she wouldn't look at it. Said she wanted to die. He got quite uneasy till 'e came 'ome the next night and found the best part of a loaf o' bread, a quarter o' butter, and a couple o' chops he 'ad got in for 'is supper had gorn; and then when he said 'e was glad she 'ad got 'er appetite back she turned round and said that he grudged 'er the food she ate.

And no woman ever owned up as 'ow she was wrong; and the more you try and prove it to 'em the louder they talk about something else. I know wot I'm talking about because a woman made a mistake about me once, and though she was proved to be in the wrong, and it was years ago, my missus shakes her 'ead about it to this day.

It was about eight years arter I 'ad left off going to sea and took up night-watching. A beautiful summer evening it was, and I was sitting by the gate smoking a pipe till it should be time to light up, when I noticed a woman who 'ad just passed turn back and stand staring at me. I've 'ad that sort o' thing before, and I went on smoking and looking straight in front of me. Fat middle-aged woman she was, wot 'ad lost her good looks and found others. She stood there staring and staring, and by and by she tries a little cough.

I got up very slow then, and, arter looking all round at the evening, without seeing 'er, I was just going to step inside and shut the wicket, when she came closer.

"Bill!" she ses, in a choking sort o' voice.

"Bill!"

I gave her a look that made her catch 'er breath, and I was just stepping through the wicket, when she laid hold of my coat and tried to hold me back.

"Do you know wot you're a-doing of?" I ses, turning on her.

"Oh, Bill dear," she ses, "don't talk to me like that. Do you want to break my 'art? Arter all these years!"

She pulled out a dirt-coloured pocket-'ankercher and stood there dabbing her eyes with it. One eye at a time she dabbed, while she looked at me reproachful with the other. And arter eight dabs, four to each eye, she began to sob as if her 'art would break.

"Go away," I ses, very slow. "You can't stand making that noise outside my wharf. Go away and give somebody else a treat."

Afore she could say anything the potman from the Tiger, a nasty ginger- 'aired little chap that nobody liked, come by and stopped to pat her on the back.

"There, there, don't take on, mother," he ses. "Wot's he been a-doing to you?"

"You get off 'ome," I ses, losing my temper.

"Wot d'ye mean trying to drag me into it? I've never seen the woman afore in my life."

"Oh, Bill!" ses the woman, sobbing louder than ever. "Oh! Oh! Oh!"

"'Ow does she know your name, then?" ses the little beast of a potman.

I didn't answer him. I might have told 'im that there's about five million Bills in England, but I didn't. I stood there with my arms folded acrost my chest, and looked at him, superior.

"Where 'ave you been all this long, long time?" she ses, between her sobs. "Why did you leave your happy 'ome and your children wot loved you?"

The potman let off a whistle that you could have 'eard acrost the river, and as for me, I thought I should ha' dropped. To have a woman standing sobbing and taking my character away like that was a'most more than I could bear.

"Did he run away from you?" ses the potman.

"Ye-ye-yes," she ses. "He went off on a vy'ge to China over nine years ago, and that's the last I saw of 'im till to-night. A lady friend o' mine thought she reck-ernized 'im yesterday, and told me."

"I shouldn't cry over 'im," ses the potman, shaking his 'ead: "he ain't worth it. If I was you I should just give 'im a bang or two over the 'ead with my umberella, and then give 'im in charge."

I stepped inside the wicket--backwards--and then I slammed it in their faces, and putting the key in my pocket, walked up the wharf. I knew it was no good standing out there argufying. I felt sorry for the pore thing in a way. If she really thought I was her 'usband, and she 'ad lost me---- I put one or two things straight and then, for the sake of distracting my mind, I 'ad a word or two with the skipper of the John Henry, who was leaning against the side of his ship, smoking.

"Wot's that tapping noise?" he ses, all of a sudden. "'Ark!"

I knew wot it was. It was the handle of that umberella 'ammering on the gate. I went cold all over, and then when I thought that the pot-man was most likely encouraging 'er to do it I began to boil.

"Somebody at the gate," ses the skipper.

"Aye, aye," I ses. "I know all about it."

I went on talking until at last the skipper asked me whether he was wandering in 'is mind, or whether I was. The mate came up from the cabin just then, and o' course he 'ad to tell me there was somebody knocking at the gate.

"Ain't you going to open it?" ses the skipper, staring at me.

"Let 'em ring," I ses, off-hand.

The words was 'ardly out of my mouth afore they did ring, and if they 'ad been selling muffins they couldn't ha' kept it up harder. And all the time the umberella was doing rat-a-tat tats on the gate, while a voice-- much too loud for the potman's--started calling out: "Watch-man ahoy!"

"They're calling you, Bill," ses the skipper. "I ain't deaf," I ses, very cold.

"Well, I wish I was," ses the skipper. "It's fair making my ear ache. Why the blazes don't you do your dooty, and open the gate?"

"You mind your bisness and I'll mind mine," I ses. "I know wot I'm doing. It's just some silly fools 'aving a game with me, and I'm not going to encourage 'em."

"Game with you?" ses the skipper. "Ain't they got anything better than that to play with? Look 'ere, if you don't open that gate, I will."

"It's nothing to do with you," I ses. "You look arter your ship and I'll look arter my wharf. See? If you don't like the noise, go down in the cabin and stick your 'ead in a biscuit-bag."

To my surprise he took the mate by the arm and went, and I was just thinking wot a good thing it was to be a bit firm with people sometimes, when they came back dressed up in their coats and bowler-hats and climbed on to the wharf.

"Watchman!" ses the skipper, in a hoity-toity sort o' voice, "me and the mate is going as far as Aldgate for a breath o' fresh air. Open the gate."

I gave him a look that might ha' melted a 'art of stone, and all it done to 'im was to make 'im laugh.

"Hurry up," he ses. "It a'most seems to me that there's somebody ringing the bell, and you can let them in same time as you let us out. Is it the bell, or is it my fancy, Joe?" he ses, turning to the mate.

They marched on in front of me with their noses cocked in the air, and all the time the noise at the gate got worse and worse. So far as I could make out, there was quite a crowd outside, and I stood there with the key in the lock, trembling all over. Then I unlocked it very careful, and put my hand on the skipper's arm.

"Nip out quick," I ses, in a whisper.

"I'm in no hurry," ses the skipper. "Here! Halloa, wot's up?"

It was like opening the door at a theatre, and the fust one through was that woman, shoved behind by the potman. Arter 'im came a car-man, two big 'ulking brewers' draymen, a little scrap of a woman with 'er bonnet cocked over one eye, and a couple of dirty little boys.

"Wot is it?" ses the skipper, shutting the wicket behind 'em. "A beanfeast?"

"This lady wants her 'usband," ses the pot-man, pointing at me. "He run away from her nine years ago, and now he says he 'as never seen 'er before. He ought to be 'ung."

"Bill," ses the skipper, shaking his silly 'ead at me. "I can 'ardly believe it."

"It's all a pack o' silly lies," I ses, firing up. "She's made a mistake."

"She made a mistake when she married you," ses the thin little woman. "If I was in 'er shoes I'd take 'old of you and tear you limb from limb."

"I don't want to hurt 'im, ma'am," ses the other woman. "I on'y want him to come 'ome to me and my five. Why, he's never seen the youngest, little Annie. She's as like 'im as two peas."

"Pore little devil," ses the carman.

"Look here!" I ses, "you clear off. All of you. 'Ow dare you come on to my wharf? If you aren't gone in two minutes I'll give you all in charge."

"Who to?" ses one of the draymen, sticking his face into mine. "You go 'ome to your wife and kids. Go on now, afore I put up my 'ands to you."

"That's the way to talk to 'im," ses the pot-man, nodding at 'em.

They all began to talk to me then and tell me wot I was to do, and wot they would do if I didn't. I couldn't get a word in edgeways. When I reminded the mate that when he was up in London 'e always passed himself off as a single man, 'e wouldn't listen; and when I asked the skipper whether 'is pore missus was blind, he on'y went on shouting at the top of 'is voice. It on'y showed me 'ow anxious most people are that everybody else should be good.

I thought they was never going to stop, and, if it 'adn't been for a fit of coughing, I don't believe that the scraggy little woman could ha' stopped. Arter one o' the draymen 'ad saved her life and spoilt 'er temper by patting 'er on the back with a hand the size of a leg o' mutton, the carman turned to me and told me to tell the truth, if it choked me.

"I have told you the truth," I ses. "She ses I'm her 'usband and I say I ain't. Ow's she going to prove it? Why should you believe her, and not me?"

"She's got a truthful face," ses the carman.

"Look here!" ses the skipper, speaking very slow, "I've got an idea, wot'll settle it p'raps. You get outside," he ses, turning sharp on the two little boys.

One o' the draymen 'elped 'em to go out, and 'arf a minute arterwards a stone came over the gate and cut the potman's lip open. Boys will be boys.

"Now!" ses the skipper, turning to the woman, and smiling with conceitedness. "Had your 'usband got any marks on 'im? Birth-mark, or moles, or anything of that sort?"

"I'm sure he is my 'usband," ses the woman, dabbing her eyes.

"Yes, yes," ses the skipper, "but answer my question. If you can tell us any marks your 'usband had, we can take Bill down into my cabin and----"

"You'll do WOT?" I ses, in a loud voice.

"You speak when you're spoke to," ses the carman. "It's got nothing to do with you."

"No, he ain't got no birthmarks," ses the woman, speaking very slow--and I could see she was afraid of making a mistake and losing me--"but he's got tattoo marks. He's got a mermaid tattooed on 'im."

"Where?" ses the skipper, a'most jumping.

I 'eld my breath. Five sailormen out of ten have been tattooed with mermaids, and I was one of 'em. When she spoke agin I thought I should ha' dropped.

"On 'is right arm," she ses, "unless he's 'ad it rubbed off."

"You can't rub out tattoo marks," ses the skipper.

They all stood looking at me as if they was waiting for something. I folded my arms--tight--and stared back at 'em.

"If you ain't this lady's 'usband," ses the skipper, turning to me, "you can take off your coat and prove it."

"And if you don't we'll take it off for you," ses the carman, coming a bit closer.

Arter that things 'appened so quick, I hardly knew whether I was standing on my 'cad or my heels. Both, I think. They was all on top o' me at once, and the next thing I can remember is sitting on the ground in my shirt-sleeves listening to the potman, who was making a fearful fuss because somebody 'ad bit his ear 'arf off. My coat was ripped up the back, and one of the draymen was holding up my arm and showing them all the mermaid, while the other struck matches so as they could see better."

"That's your 'usband right enough," he ses to the woman. "Take 'im."

"P'raps she'll carry 'im 'ome," I ses, very fierce and sarcastic.

"And we don't want none of your lip," ses the carman, who was in a bad temper because he 'ad got a fearful kick on the shin from somewhere.

I got up very slow and began to put my coat on again, and twice I 'ad to tell that silly woman that when I wanted her 'elp I'd let 'er know. Then I 'eard slow, heavy footsteps in the road outside, and, afore any of 'em could stop me, I was calling for the police.

I don't like policemen as a rule; they're too inquisitive, but when the wicket was pushed open and I saw a face with a helmet on it peeping in, I felt quite a liking for 'em.

"Wot's up?" ses the policeman, staring 'ard at my little party.

They all started telling 'im at once, and I should think if the potman showed him 'is ear once he showed it to 'im twenty times. He lost his temper and pushed it away at last, and the potman gave a 'owl that set my teeth on edge. I waited till they was all finished, and the policeman trying to get 'is hearing back, and then I spoke up in a quiet way and told 'im to clear them all off of my wharf.

"They're trespassing," I ses, "all except the skipper and mate here. They belong to a little wash-tub that's laying alongside, and they're both as 'armless as they look."

It's wonderful wot a uniform will do. The policeman just jerked his 'ead and said "out-side," and the men went out like a flock of sheep. The on'y man that said a word was the carman, who was in such a hurry that 'e knocked his bad shin against my foot as 'e went by. The thin little woman was passed out by the policeman in the middle of a speech she was making, and he was just going for the other, when the skipper stopped 'im.

"This lady is coming on my ship," he ses, puffing out 'is chest.

I looked at 'im, and then I turned to the policeman. "So long as she goes off my wharf, I don't mind where she goes," I ses. "The skipper's goings-on 'ave got nothing to do with me."

"Then she can foller him 'ome in the morning," ses the skipper. "Good night, watch-man."

Him and the mate 'elped the silly old thing to the ship, and, arter I 'ad been round to the Bear's Head and fetched a pint for the police-man, I locked up and sat down to think things out; and the more I thought the worse they seemed. I've 'eard people say that if you have a clear conscience nothing can hurt you. They didn't know my missus.

I got up at last and walked on to the jetty, and the woman, wot was sitting on the deck of the John Henry, kept calling out: "Bill!" like a sick baa-lamb crying for its ma. I went back, and 'ad four pints at the Bear's Head, but it didn't seem to do me any good, and at last I went and sat down in the office to wait for morning.

It came at last, a lovely morning with a beautiful sunrise; and that woman sitting up wide awake, waiting to foller me 'ome. When I opened the gate at six o'clock she was there with the mate and the skipper, waiting, and when I left at five minutes past she was trotting along beside me.

Twice I stopped and spoke to 'er, but it was no good. Other people stopped too, and I 'ad to move on agin; and every step was bringing me nearer to my house and the missus.

I turned into our street, arter passing it three times, and the first thing I saw was my missus standing on the doorstep 'aving a few words with the lady next door. Then she 'appened to look up and see us, just as that silly woman was trying to walk arm-in-arm.

Twice I knocked her 'and away, and then, right afore my wife and the party next door, she put her arm round my waist. By the time I got to the 'ouse my legs was trembling so I could hardly stand, and when I got into the passage I 'ad to lean up against the wall for a bit.

"Keep 'er out," I ses.

"Wot do you want?" ses my missus, trembling with passion. "Wot do you think you're doing?"

"I want my 'usband, Bill," ses the woman.

My missus put her 'and to her throat and came in without a word, and the woman follered 'er. If I hadn't kept my presence o' mind and shut the door two or three more would 'ave come in too.

I went into the kitchen about ten minutes arterwards to see 'ow they was getting on. Besides which they was both calling for me.

"Now then!" ses my missus, who was leaning up against the dresser with 'er arms folded, "wot 'ave you got to say for yourself walking in as bold as brass with

RIGHT AFORE MY WIFE AND THE PARTY NEXT DOOR SHE PUT HER
ARM ROUND MY WAIST.

this hussy?"

"Bill!" ses the woman, "did you hear wot she called me?"

She spoke to me like that afore my wife, and in two minutes they was at it, hammer and tongs.

Fust of all they spoke about each other, and then my missus started speaking about me. She's got a better memory than most people, because she can remember things that never 'appened, and every time I coughed she turned on me like a tiger.

"And as for you," she ses, turning to the woman, "if you did marry 'im you should ha' made sure that he 'adn't got a wife already."

"He married me fust," ses the woman.

"When?" ses my wife. "Wot was the date?"

"Wot was the date you married 'im?" ses the other one.

They stood looking at each other like a couple o' game-cocks, and I could see as plain as a pike-staff 'ow frightened both of 'em was o' losing me.

"Look here!" I ses at last, to my missus, "talk sense. 'Ow could I be married to 'er? When I was at sea I was at sea, and when I was ashore I was with you."

"Did you use to go down to the ship to see 'im off?" ses the woman.

"No," ses my wife. "I'd something better to do."

"Neither did I," ses the woman. "P'raps that's where we both made a mistake."

"You get out of my 'ouse!" ses my missus, very sudden. "Go on, afore I put you out."

"Not without my Bill," ses the woman. "If you lay a finger on me I'll scream the house down."

"You brought her 'ere," ses my wife, turning to me, "now you can take 'er away?"

"I didn't bring 'er," I ses. "She follered me."

"Well, she can foller you agin," she ses. "Go on!" she ses, trembling all over. "Git out afore I start on you."

I was in such a temper that I daren't trust myself to stop. I just gave 'er one look, and then I drew myself up and went out. 'Alf the fools in our street was standing in front of the 'ouse, 'umming like bees, but I took no notice. I held my 'ead up and walked through them with that woman trailing arter me.

I was in such a state of mind that I went on like a man in a dream. If it had ha' been a dream I should ha' pushed 'er under an omnibus, but you can't do things like that in real life.

"Penny for your thoughts, Bill," she ses. I didn't answer her.

"Why don't you speak to me?" she ses.

"You don't know wot you're asking for," I ses.

I was hungry and sleepy, and 'ow I was going to get through the day I couldn't think. I went into a pub and 'ad a couple o' pints o' stout and a crust o' bread and cheese for brekfuss. I don't know wot she 'ad, but when the barman tried to take for it out o' my money, I surprised 'im.

We walked about till I was ready to drop. Then we got to Victoria Park, and I 'ad no sooner got on to the grass than I laid down and went straight off to sleep. It was two o'clock when I woke, and, arter a couple o' pork-pies and a pint or two, I sat on a seat in the Park smoking, while she kep' dabbing 'er eyes agin and asking me to come 'ome.

At five o'clock I got up to go back to the wharf, and, taking no notice of 'er, I walked into the street and jumped on a 'bus that was passing. She jumped too, and, arter the conductor had 'elped 'er up off of 'er knees and taken her arms away from his waist, I'm blest if he didn't turn on me and ask me why I 'adn't left her at 'ome.

We got to the wharf just afore six. The John Henry 'ad gorn, but the skipper 'ad done all the 'arm he could afore he sailed, and, if I 'adn't kept my temper, I should ha' murdered arf a dozen of 'em.

The woman wanted to come on to the wharf, but I 'ad a word or two with one o' the fore-men, who owed me arf-a-dollar, and he made that all right.

"We all 'ave our faults, Bill," he ses as 'e went out, "and I suppose she was better looking once upon a time?"

I didn't answer 'im. I shut the wicket arter 'im, quick, and turned the key, and then I went on with my work. For a long time everything was as quiet as the grave, and then there came just one little pull at the bell. Five minutes arterwards there was another.

I thought it was that woman, but I 'ad to make sure. When it came the third time I crept up to the gate.

"Halloa!" I ses. "Who is it?"

"Me, darling," ses a voice I reckernized as the potman's. "Your missus wants to come in and sit down."

I could 'ear several people talking, and it seemed to me there was quite a crowd out there, and by and by that bell was going like mad. Then people started kicking the gate, and shouting, but I took no notice until, presently, it left off all of a sudden, and I 'eard a loud voice asking what it was all about. I suppose there was about fifty of 'em all telling it at once, and then there was the sound of a fist on the gate.

"Who is it?" I ses.

"Police," ses the voice.

I opened the wicket then and looked out. A couple o' policemen was standing by the gate and arf the riff-raff of Wapping behind 'em.

"Wot's all this about?" ses one o' the policemen.

I shook my 'ead. "Ask me another," I ses. "Your missus is causing a disturbance," he ses.

"She's not my missus," I ses; "she's a complete stranger to me."

"And causing a crowd to collect and refusing to go away," ses the other policeman.

"That's your business," I ses. "It's nothing to do with me."

They talked to each other for a moment, and then they spoke to the woman. I didn't 'ear wot she said, but I saw her shake her 'ead, and a'most direckly arterwards she was marching away between the two policemen with the crowd follering and advising 'er where to kick 'em.

I was a bit worried at fust--not about her--and then I began to think that p'raps it was the best thing that could have 'appened.

I went 'ome in the morning with a load lifted off my mind; but I 'adn't been in the 'ouse two seconds afore my missus started to put it on agin. Fust of all she asked me 'ow I dared to come into the 'ouse, and then she wanted to know wot I meant by leaving her at 'ome and going out for the day with another woman.

"You told me to," I ses.

"Oh, yes," she ses, trembling with temper. "You always do wot I tell you, don't you? Al-ways 'ave, especially when it's anything you like."

She fetched a bucket o' water and scrubbed the kitchen while I was having my brekfuss, but I kept my eye on 'er, and, the moment she 'ad finished, I did the perlite and emptied the bucket for 'er, to prevent mistakes.

I read about the case in the Sunday paper, and I'm thankful to say my name wasn't in it. All the magistrate done was to make 'er promise that she wouldn't do it again, and then he let 'er go. I should ha' felt more comfortable if he 'ad given 'er five years, but, as it turned out, it didn't matter. Her 'usband happened to read it, and, whether 'e was tired of living alone, or whether he was excited by 'caring that she 'ad got a little general shop, 'e went back to her.

The fust I knew about it was they came round to the wharf to see me. He 'ad been a fine-looking chap in 'is day, and even then 'e was enough like me for me to see 'ow she 'ad made the mistake; and all the time she was telling me 'ow it 'appened, he was looking me up and down and sniffing.

"'Ave you got a cold?" I ses, at last.

"Wot's that got to do with you?" he ses. "Wot do you mean by walking out with my wife? That's what I've come to talk about."

For a moment I thought that his bad luck 'ad turned 'is brain. "You've got it wrong," I ses, as soon as I could speak. "She walked out with me."

"Cos she thought you was her 'usband," he ses, "but you didn't think you was me, did you?"

"'Course I didn't," I ses.

"Then 'ow dare you walk out with 'er?" he ses.

"Look 'ere!" I ses. "You get off 'ome as quick as you like. I've 'ad about enough of your family. Go on, hook it."

Afore I could put my 'ands up he 'it me hard in the mouth, and the next moment we was at it as 'ard as we could go. Nearly every time I hit 'im he wasn't there, and every time 'e hit me I wished I hadn't ha' been. When I said I had 'ad enough, 'e contradicted me and kept on, but he got tired of it at last, and, arter telling me wot he would do if I ever walked 'is wife out agin, they went off like a couple o' love-birds.

By the time I got 'ome next morning my eyes was so swelled up I could 'ardly see, and my nose wouldn't let me touch it. I was so done up I could 'ardly speak, but I managed to tell my missus about it arter I had 'ad a cup o' tea. Judging by her face anybody might ha' thought I was telling 'er something funny, and, when I 'ad finished, she looks up at the ceiling and ses:

"I 'ope it'll be a lesson to you," she ses.

A GOLDEN VENTURE

The elders of the Tidger family sat at breakfast--Mrs. Tidger with knees wide apart and the youngest Tidger nestling in the valley of print-dress which lay between, and Mr. Tidger bearing on one moleskin knee a small copy of himself in a red flannel frock and a slipper. The larger Tidger children took the solids of their breakfast up and down the stone-flagged court outside, coming in occasionally to gulp draughts of very weak tea from a gallipot or two which stood on the table, and to wheedle Mr. Tidger out of any small piece of bloater which he felt generous enough to bestow.

"Peg away, Ann," said Mr. Tidger, heartily.

His wife's elder sister shook her head, and passing the remains of her slice to one of her small nephews, leaned back in her chair. "No appetite, Tidger," she said, slowly.

"You should go in for carpentering," said Mr. Tidger, in justification of the huge crust he was carving into mouthfuls with his pocket-knife. "Seems to me I can't eat enough sometimes. Hullo, who's the letter for?"

He took it from the postman, who stood at the door amid a bevy of Tidgers who had followed him up the court, and slowly read the address.

"'Mrs. Ann Pullen,'" he said, handing it over to his sister-in-law; "nice writing, too."

Mrs. Pullen broke the envelope, and after a somewhat lengthy search for her pocket, fumbled therein for her spectacles. She then searched the mantelpiece, the chest of drawers, and the dresser, and finally ran them to earth on the copper.

She was not a good scholar, and it took her some time to read the letter, a proceeding which she punctuated with such "Ohs" and "Ahs" and gaspings and "God bless my souls" as nearly drove the carpenter and his wife, who were leaning forward impatiently, to the verge of desperation.

"Who's it from?" asked Mr. Tidger for the third time.

"I don't know," said Mrs. Pullen. "Good gracious, who ever would ha' thought it!"

"Thought what, Ann?" demanded the carpenter, feverishly.

"Why don't people write their names plain?" demanded his sister-in-law, impatiently. "It's got a printed name up in the corner; perhaps that's it. Well, I never did--I don't know whether I'm standing on my head or my heels."

"You're sitting down, that's what you're a-doing," said the carpenter, regarding her somewhat unfavourably.

"Perhaps it's a take-in," said Mrs. Pullen, her lips trembling. "I've heard o' such things. If it is, I shall never get over it--never."

"Get--over--what?" asked the carpenter.

"It don't look like a take-in," soliloquized Mrs. Pullen, "and I shouldn't think anybody'd go to all that trouble and spend a penny to take in a poor thing like me."

Mr. Tidger, throwing politeness to the winds, leaped forward, and snatching the letter from her, read it with feverish haste, tempered by a defective education.

"It's a take-in, Ann," he said, his voice trembling; "it must be."

"What is?" asked Mrs. Tidger, impatiently.

"Looks like it," said Mrs. Pullen, feebly.

"What is it?" screamed Mrs. Tidger, wrought beyond all endurance.

Her husband turned and regarded her with much severity, but Mrs. Tidger's gaze was the stronger, and after a vain attempt to meet it, he handed her the letter.

Mrs. Tidger read it through hastily, and then snatching the baby from her lap, held it out with both arms to her husband, and jumping up, kissed her sister heartily, patting her on the back in her excitement until she coughed with the pain of it.

"You don't think it's a take-in, Polly?" she inquired.

"Take-in?" said her sister; "of course it ain't. Lawyers don't play jokes; their time's too valuable. No, you're an heiress all right, Ann, and I wish you joy. I couldn't be more pleased if it was myself."

She kissed her again, and going to pat her back once more, discovered that she had sunk down sufficiently low in her chair to obtain the protection of its back.

"Two thousand pounds," said Mrs. Pullen, in an awestruck voice.

"Ten hundered pounds twice over," said the carpenter, mouthing it slowly; "twenty hundered pounds."

He got up from the table, and instinctively realizing that he could not do full justice to his feelings with the baby in his arms, laid it on the teatray in a puddle of cold tea and stood looking hard at the heiress.

"I was housekeeper to her eleven years ago," said Mrs. Pullen. "I wonder what she left it to me for?"

"Didn't know what to do with it, I should think," said the carpenter, still staring openmouthed.

"Tidger, I'm ashamed of you," said his wife, snatching her infant to her bosom. "I expect you was very good to her, Ann."

"I never 'ad no luck," said the impenitent carpenter. "Nobody ever left me no money. Nobody ever left me so much as a fi-pun note."

He stared round disdainfully at his poor belongings, and drawing on his coat, took his bag from a corner, and hoisting it on his shoulder, started to his work. He scattered the news as he went, and it ran up and down the little main street of Thatcham, and thence to the outlying lanes and cottages. Within a couple of hours it was common property, and the fortunate legatee was presented with a congratulatory address every time she ventured near the door.

It is an old adage that money makes friends; the carpenter was surprised to find that the mere fact of his having a moneyed relation had the same effect, and that men to whom he had hitherto shown a certain amount of respect due to their position now sought his company. They stood him beer at the "Bell," and walked by his side through the street. When they took to dropping in of an evening to smoke a pipe the carpenter was radiant with happiness.

"You don't seem to see beyond the end of your nose, Tidger," said the wife of his bosom after they had retired one evening.

"H'm?" said the startled carpenter.

"What do you think old Miller, the dealer, comes here for?" demanded his wife.

"Smoke his pipe," replied her husband, confidently.

"And old Wiggett?" persisted Mrs. Tidger.

"Smoke his pipe," was the reply. "Why, what's the matter, Polly?"

Mrs. Tidger sniffed derisively. "You men are all alike," she snapped. "What do you think Ann wears that pink bodice for?"

"I never noticed she 'ad a pink bodice, Polly," said the carpenter.

"No? That's what I say. You men never notice anything," said his wife. "If you don't send them two old fools off, I will."

"Don't you like 'em to see Ann wearing pink?" inquired the mystified Tidger.

Mrs. Tidger bit her lip and shook her head at him scornfully. "In plain English, Tidger, as plain as I can speak it,"--she said, severely, "they're after Ann and 'er bit o' money."

Mr. Tidger gazed at her open-mouthed, and taking advantage of that fact, blew out the candle to hide his discomposure. "What!" he said, blankly, "at 'er time o' life?"

"Watch 'em to-morrer," said his wife.

The carpenter acted upon his instructions, and his ire rose as he noticed the assiduous attention paid by his two friends to the frivolous Mrs. Pullen. Mr. Wiggett, a sharp-featured little man, was doing most of the talking, while his rival, a stout, clean-shaven man with a slow, oxlike eye, looked on stolidly. Mr. Miller was seldom in a hurry, and lost many a bargain through his slowness--a fact which sometimes so painfully affected the individual who had outdistanced him that he would offer to let him have it at a still lower figure.

"You get younger than ever, Mrs. Pullen," said Wiggett, the conversation having turned upon ages.

"Young ain't the word for it," said Miller, with a praiseworthy determination not to be left behind.

"No; it's age as you're thinking of, Mr. Wiggett," said the carpenter, slowly; "none of us gets younger, do we, Ann?"

"Some of us keeps young in our ways," said Mrs. Pullen, somewhat shortly.

"How old should you say Ann is now?" persisted the watchful Tidger.

Mr. Wiggett shook his head. "I should say she's about fifteen years younger nor me," he said, slowly, "and I'm as lively as a cricket."

"YOU GET YOUNGER THAN EVER, MRS. PULLEN."

"She's fifty-five," said the carpenter.

"That makes you seventy, Wiggett," said Mr. Miller, pointedly. "I thought you was more than that. You look it."

Mr. Wiggett coughed sourly. "I'm fifty-nine," he growled. "Nothing 'll make me believe as Mrs. Pullen's fifty-five, nor anywhere near it."

"Ho!" said the carpenter, on his mettle--"ho! Why, my wife here was the sixth child, and she---- He caught a gleam in the sixth child's eye, and expressed her age with a cough. The others waited politely until he had finished, and Mr. Tidger, noticing this, coughed again.

"And she--" prompted Mr. Miller, displaying a polite interest.

"She ain't so young as she was," said the carpenter.

"Cares of a family," said Mr. Wiggett, plumping boldly. "I always thought Mrs. Pullen was younger than her."

"So did I," said Mr. Miller, "much younger."

Mr. Wiggett eyed him sharply. It was rather hard to have Miller hiding his lack of invention by participating in his compliments and even improving upon them. It was the way he dealt at market-listening to other dealers' accounts of their wares, and adding to them for his own.

"I was noticing you the other day, ma'am," continued Mr. Wiggett. "I see you going up the road with a step free and easy as a young girl's."

"She allus walks like that," said Mr. Miller, in a tone of surprised reproof.

"It's in the family," said the carpenter, who had been uneasily watching his wife's face.

"Both of you seem to notice a lot," said Mrs. Tidger; "much more than you used to."

Mr. Tidger, who was of a nervous and sensitive disposition, coughed again.

"You ought to take something for that cough," said Mr. Wiggett, considerately.

"Gin and beer," said Mr. Miller, with the air of a specialist.

"Bed's the best thing for it," said Mrs. Tidger, whose temper was beginning to show signs of getting out of hand.

Mr. Tidger rose and looked awkwardly at his visitors; Mr. Wiggett got up, and pretending to notice the time, said he must be going, and looked at Mr. Miller. That gentleman, who was apparently deep in some knotty problem, was gazing at the floor, and oblivious for the time to his surroundings.

"Come along," said Wiggett, with feigned heartiness, slapping him on the back.

Mr. Miller, looking for a moment as though he would like to return the compliment, came back to everyday life, and bidding the company good-night, stepped to the door, accompanied by his rival. It was immediately shut with some violence.

"They seem in a hurry," said Wiggett. "I don't think I shall go there again."

"I don't think I shall," said Mr. Miller.

After this neither of them was surprised to meet there again the next night, and indeed for several nights. The carpenter and his wife, who did not want the money to go out of the family, and were also afraid of offending Mrs. Pullen, were at their wits' end what to do. Ultimately it was resolved that Tidger, in as delicate a manner as possible, was to hint to her that they were after her money. He was so vague and so delicate that Mrs. Pullen misunderstood him, and fancying that he was trying to borrow half a crown, made him a present of five shillings.

It was evident to the slower-going Mr. Miller that his rival's tongue was giving him an advantage which only the ever-watchful presence of the carpenter and his wife prevented him from pushing to the fullest advantage. In these circumstances he sat for two hours after breakfast one morning in deep cogitation, and after six pipes got up with a twinkle in his slow eyes which his brother dealers had got to regard as a danger signal.

He had only the glimmering of an idea at first, but after a couple of pints at the "Bell" everything took shape, and he cast his eyes about for an assistant. They fell upon a man named Smith, and the dealer, after some thought, took up his glass and went over to him.

"I want you to do something for me," he remarked, in a mysterious voice.

"Ah, I've been wanting to see you," said Smith, who was also a dealer in a small way. "One o' them hins I bought off you last week is dead."

"I'll give you another for it," said Miller.

"And the others are so forgetful," continued Mr. Smith.

"Forgetful?" repeated the other.

"Forget to lay, like," said Mr. Smith, musingly.

"Never mind about them," said Mr. Miller, with some animation. "I want you to do something for me. If it comes off all right, I'll give you a dozen hins and a couple of decentish-sized pigs."

Mr. Smith called a halt. "Decentish-sized" was vague.

"Take your pick," said Mr. Miller. "You know Mrs. Pullen's got two thousand pounds--"

"Wiggett's going to have it," said the other; "he as good as told me so."

"He's after her money," said the other, sadly. "Look 'ere, Smith, I want you to tell him she's lost it all. Say that Tidger told you, but you wasn't to tell anybody else. Wiggett 'll believe you."

Mr. Smith turned upon him a face all wrinkles, lit by one eye. "I want the hins and the pigs first," he said, firmly.

Mr. Miller, shocked at his grasping spirit, stared at him mournfully.

"And twenty pounds the day you marry Mrs. Pullen," continued Mr. Smith.

Mr. Miller, leading him up and down the sawdust floor, besought him to listen to reason, and Mr. Smith allowed the better feelings of our common human nature to prevail to the extent of reducing his demands to half a dozen fowls on account, and all the rest on the day of the marriage. Then, with the delightful feeling that he wouldn't do any work for a week, he went out to drop poison into the ears of Mr. Wiggett.

"Lost all her money!" said the startled Mr. Wiggett. "How?"

"I don't know how," said his friend. "Tidger told me, but made me promise not to tell a soul. But I couldn't help telling you, Wiggett, 'cause I know what you're after."

"Do me a favour," said the little man.

"I will," said the other.

"Keep it from Miller as long as possible. If you hear any one else talking of it, tell 'em to keep it from him. If he marries her I'll give you a couple of pints."

Mr. Smith promised faithfully, and both the Tidgers and Mrs. Pullen were surprised to find that Mr. Miller was the only visitor that evening. He spoke but little, and that little in a slow, ponderous voice intended for Mrs. Pullen's ear alone. He spoke disparagingly of money, and shook his head slowly at the temptations it brought in its train. Give him a crust, he said, and somebody to halve it with--a home-made crust baked by a wife. It was a pretty picture, but somewhat spoiled by Mrs. Tidger suggesting that, though he had spoken of halving the crust, he had said nothing about the beer.

"Half of my beer wouldn't be much," said the dealer, slowly.

"Not the half you would give your wife wouldn't," retorted Mrs. Tidger.

The dealer sighed and looked mournfully at Mrs. Pullen. The lady sighed in return, and finding that her admirer's stock of conversation seemed to be exhausted, coyly suggested a game of draughts. The dealer assented with eagerness, and declining the offer of a glass of beer by explaining that he had had one the day before yesterday, sat down and lost seven games right off. He gave up at the seventh game, and pushing back his chair, said that he thought Mrs. Pullen was the most wonderful draught- player he had ever seen, and took no notice when Mrs. Tidger, in a dry voice charged with subtle meaning, said that she thought he was.

"Draughts come natural to some people," said Mrs. Pullen, modestly. "It's as easy as kissing your fingers."

Mr. Miller looked doubtful; then he put his great fingers to his lips by way of experiment, and let them fall unmistakably in the widow's direction. Mrs. Pullen looked down and nearly blushed. The carpenter and his wife eyed each other in indignant consternation.

"That's easy enough," said the dealer, and repeated the offense.

Mrs. Pullen got up in some confusion, and began to put the draught-board away. One of the pieces fell on the floor, and as they both stooped to recover it their heads bumped. It was nothing to the dealer's, but Mrs. Pullen rubbed hers and sat down with her eyes watering. Mr. Miller took out his handkerchief, and going to the scullery, dipped it into water and held it to her head.

"Is it better?" he inquired.

"A little better," said the victim, with a shiver.

Mr. Miller, in his emotion, was squeezing the handkerchief hard, and a cold stream was running down her neck.

"Thank you. It's all right now."

The dealer replaced the handkerchief, and sat for some time regarding her earnestly. Then the carpenter and his wife displaying manifest signs of impatience, he took his departure, after first inviting himself for another game of draughts the following night.

He walked home with the air of a conqueror, and thought exultingly that the two thousand pounds were his. It was a deal after his own heart, and not the least satisfactory part about it was the way he had got the better of Wiggett.

He completed his scheme the following day after a short interview with the useful Smith. By the afternoon Wiggett found that his exclusive information was common property, and all Thatcham was marvelling at the fortitude with which Mrs. Pullen was bearing the loss of her fortune. With a view of being out of the way when the denial was published, Mr. Miller, after loudly expressing in public his sympathy for Mrs. Pullen and his admiration of her qualities, drove over with some pigs to a neighbouring village, returning to Thatcham in the early evening. Then hurriedly putting his horse up he made his way to the carpenter's.

The Tidgers were at home when he entered, and Mrs. Pullen flushed faintly as he shook hands.

"I was coming in before," he said, impressively, "after what I heard this afternoon, but I had to drive over to Thorpe."

"You 'eard it?" inquired the carpenter, in an incredulous voice.

"Certainly," said the dealer, "and very sorry I was. Sorry for one thing, but glad for another."

The carpenter opened his mouth and seemed about to speak. Then he checked himself suddenly and gazed with interest at the ingenuous dealer.

"I'm glad," said Mr. Miller, slowly, as he nodded at a friend of Mrs. Tidger's who had just come in with a long face, "because now that Mrs. Pullen is poor, I can say to her what I couldn't say while she was rich."

Again the astonished carpenter was about to speak, but the dealer hastily checked him with his hand.

"One at a time," he said. "Mrs. Pullen, I was very sorry to hear this afternoon, for your sake, that you had lost all your money. What I wanted to say to you now, now that you are poor, was to ask you to be Mrs. Miller. What d'ye say?"

Mrs. Pullen, touched at so much goodness, wept softly and said, "Yes." The triumphant Miller took out his handkerchief--the same that he had used the previous night, for he was not an extravagant man--and tenderly wiped her eyes.

"Well, I'm blowed!" said the staring carpenter.

"I've got a nice little 'ouse," continued the wily Mr. Miller. "It's a poor place, but nice, and we'll play draughts every evening. When shall it be?"

"When you like," said Mrs. Pullen, in a faint voice.

"I'll put the banns up to-morrow," said the dealer.

Mrs. Tidger's lady friend giggled at so much haste, but Mrs. Tidger, who felt that she had misjudged him, was touched.

"It does you credit, Mr. Miller," she said, warmly.

"No, no," said the dealer; and then Mr. Tidger got up, and crossing the room, solemnly shook hands with him.

"Money or no money, she'll make a good wife," he said.

"I'm glad you're pleased," said the dealer, wondering at this cordiality.

"I don't deny I thought you was after her money," continued the carpenter, solemnly. "My missus thought so, too."

Mr. Miller shook his head, and said he thought they would have known him better.

"Of course it is a great loss," said the carpenter. "Money is money."

"That's all it is, though," said the slightly mystified Mr. Miller.

"What I can't understand is," continued the carpenter, "'ow the news got about. Why, the neighbours knew of it a couple of hours before we did."

The dealer hid a grin. Then he looked a bit bewildered again.

"I assure you," said the carpenter, "it was known in the town at least a couple of hours before we got the letter."

Mr. Miller waited a minute to get perfect control over his features. "Letter?" he repeated, faintly.

"The letter from the lawyers," said the carpenter.

Mr. Miller was silent again. His features were getting tiresome. He eyed the door furtively.

"What-was-in-the letter?" he asked.

"Short and sweet," said the carpenter, with bitterness. "Said it was all a mistake, because they'd been and found another will. People shouldn't make such mistakes."

"We're all liable to make mistakes," said Miller, thinking he saw an opening.

"Yes, we made a mistake when we thought you was after Ann's money," as

"WE'LL LEAVE YOU TWO YOUNG THINGS ALONE."

sented the carpenter. "I'm sure I thought you'd be the last man in the world to be pleased to hear that she'd lost it. One thing is, you've got enough for both."

Mr. Miller made no reply, but in a dazed way strove to realize the full measure of the misfortune which had befallen him. The neighbour, with the anxiety of her sex to be the first with a bit of news, had already taken her departure. He thought of Wiggett walking the earth a free man, and of Smith with a three-months' bill for twenty pounds. His pride as a dealer was shattered beyond repair, and emerging from a species of mist, he became conscious that the carpenter was addressing him.

"We'll leave you two young things alone for a bit," said Mr. Tidger, heartily. "We're going out. When you're tired o' courting you can play draughts, and Ann will show you one or two of 'er moves. So long."

CAPTAIN ROGERS

A man came slowly over the old stone bridge, and averting his gaze from the dark river with its silent craft, looked with some satisfaction toward the feeble lights of the small town on the other side. He walked with the painful, forced step of one who has already trudged far. His worsted hose, where they were not darned, were in holes, and his coat and knee-breeches were rusty with much wear, but he straightened himself as he reached the end of the bridge and stepped out bravely to the taverns which stood in a row facing the quay.

He passed the "Queen Anne"--a mere beershop--without pausing, and after a glance apiece at the "Royal George" and the "Trusty Anchor," kept on his way to where the "Golden Key" hung out a gilded emblem. It was the best house in Riverstone, and patronized by the gentry, but he adjusted his faded coat, and with a swaggering air entered and walked boldly into the coffee-room.

The room was empty, but a bright fire afforded a pleasant change to the chill October air outside. He drew up a chair, and placing his feet on the fender, exposed his tattered soles to the blaze, as a waiter who had just seen him enter the room came and stood aggressively inside the door.

"Brandy and water," said the stranger; "hot."

"The coffee-room is for gentlemen staying in the house," said the waiter.

The stranger took his feet from the fender, and rising slowly, walked toward him. He was a short man and thin, but there was something so menacing in his attitude, and something so fearsome in his stony brown eyes, that the other, despite his disgust for ill-dressed people, moved back uneasily.

"Brandy and water, hot," repeated the stranger; "and plenty of it. D'ye hear?"

The man turned slowly to depart.

"Stop!" said the other, imperiously. "What's the name of the landlord here?"

"Mullet," said the fellow, sulkily.

"Send him to me," said the other, resuming his seat; "and hark you, my friend, more civility, or 'twill be the worse for you."

He stirred the log on the fire with his foot until a shower of sparks whirled up the chimney. The door opened, and the landlord, with the waiter behind him, entered the room, but he still gazed placidly at the glowing embers.

"What do you want?" demanded the landlord, in a deep voice.

The stranger turned a little weazened yellow face and grinned at him familiarly.

"Send that fat rascal of yours away," he said, slowly.

The landlord started at his voice and eyed him closely; then he signed to the man to withdraw, and closing the door behind him, stood silently watching his visitor.

"You didn't expect to see me, Rogers," said the latter.

"My name's Mullet," said the other, sternly. "What do you want?"

"Oh, Mullet?" said the other, in surprise. "I'm afraid I've made a mistake, then. I thought you were my old shipmate, Captain Rogers. It's a foolish mistake of mine, as I've no doubt Rogers was hanged years ago. You never had a brother named Rogers, did you?"

"I say again, what do you want?" demanded the other, advancing upon him.

"Since you're so good," said the other. "I want new clothes, food, and lodging of the best, and my pockets filled with money."

"You had better go and look for all those things, then," said Mullet. "You won't find them here."

"Ay!" said the other, rising. "Well, well--There was a hundred guineas on the head of my old shipmate Rogers some fifteen years ago. I'll see whether it has been earned yet."

"If I gave you a hundred guineas," said the innkeeper, repressing his passion by a mighty effort, "you would not be satisfied."

"Reads like a book," said the stranger, in tones of pretended delight. "What a man it is!"

He fell back as he spoke, and thrusting his hand into his pocket, drew forth a long pistol as the innkeeper, a man of huge frame, edged toward him.

"Keep your distance," he said, in a sharp, quick voice.

The innkeeper, in no wise disturbed at the pistol, turned away calmly, and ringing the bell, ordered some spirits. Then taking a chair, he motioned to the other to do the same, and they sat in silence until the staring waiter had left the room again. The stranger raised his glass.

"My old friend Captain Rogers," he said, solemnly, "and may he never get his deserts!"

"From what jail have you come?" inquired Mullet, sternly.

"'Pon my soul," said the other, "I have been in so many--looking for Captain Rogers--that I almost forget the last, but I have just tramped from London, two hundred and eighty odd miles, for the pleasure of seeing your damned ugly figure-head again; and now I've found it, I'm going to stay. Give me some money."

The innkeeper, without a word, drew a little gold and silver from his pocket, and placing it on the table, pushed it toward him.

"Enough to go on with," said the other, pocketing it; "in future it is halves. D'ye hear me? Halves! And I'll stay here and see I get it."

He sat back in his chair, and meeting the other's hatred with a gaze as steady as his own, replaced his pistol.

"A nice snug harbor after our many voyages," he continued. "Shipmates we were, shipmates we'll be; while Nick Gunn is alive you shall never want for company. Lord! Do you remember the Dutch brig, and the fat frightened mate?"

"I have forgotten it," said the other, still eyeing him steadfastly. "I have forgotten many things. For fifteen years I have lived a decent, honest life. Pray God for your own sinful soul, that the devil in me does not wake again."

"Fifteen years is a long nap," said Gunn, carelessly; "what a godsend it 'll be for you to have me by you to remind you of old times! Why, you're looking smug, man; the honest innkeeper to the life! Gad! who's the girl?"

He rose and made a clumsy bow as a girl of eighteen, after a moment's hesitation at the door, crossed over to the innkeeper.

"I'm busy, my dear," said the latter, somewhat sternly.

"Our business," said Gunn, with another bow, "is finished. Is this your daughter, Rog-- Mullet?"

GUNN PLACED A HAND, WHICH LACKED
TWO FINGERS ON HIS BREAST AND BOWED AGAIN.

"My stepdaughter," was the reply.

Gunn placed a hand, which lacked two fingers, on his breast, and bowed again.

"One of your father's oldest friends," he said smoothly; "and fallen on evil days; I'm sure your gentle heart will be pleased to hear that your good father has requested me--for a time--to make his house my home."

"Any friend of my father's is welcome to me, sir," said the girl, coldly. She looked from the innkeeper to his odd-looking guest, and conscious of something strained in the air, gave him a little bow and quitted the room.

"You insist upon staying, then?" said Mullet, after a pause.

"More than ever," replied Gunn, with a leer toward the door. "Why, you don't think I'm *afraid,* Captain? You should know me better than that."

"Life is sweet," said the other.

"Ay," assented Gunn, "so sweet that you will share things with me to keep it."

"No," said the other, with great calm. "I am man enough to have a better reason."

"No psalm singing," said Gunn, coarsely. "And look cheerful, you old buccaneer. Look as a man should look who has just met an old friend never to lose him again."

He eyed his man expectantly and put his hand to his pocket again, but the innkeeper's face was troubled, and he gazed stolidly at the fire.

"See what fifteen years' honest, decent life does for us," grinned the intruder.

The other made no reply, but rising slowly, walked to the door without a word.

"Landlord," cried Gunn, bringing his maimed hand sharply down on the table.

The innkeeper turned and regarded him.

"Send me in some supper," said Gunn; "the best you have, and plenty of it, and have a room prepared. The best."

The door closed silently, and was opened a little later by the dubious George coming in to set a bountiful repast. Gunn, after cursing him for his slowness and awkwardness, drew his chair to the table and made the meal of one seldom able to satisfy his hunger. He finished at last, and after sitting for some time smoking, with his legs sprawled on the fender, rang for a candle and demanded to be shown to his room.

His proceedings when he entered it were but a poor compliment to his host. Not until he had poked and pried into every corner did he close the door. Then, not content with locking it, he tilted a chair beneath the handle, and placing his pistol beneath his pillow, fell fast asleep.

Despite his fatigue he was early astir next morning. Breakfast was laid for him in the coffee-room, and his brow darkened. He walked into the hall, and after trying various doors entered a small sitting-room, where his host and daughter sat at breakfast, and with an easy assurance drew a chair to the table. The innkeeper helped him without a word, but the girl's hand shook under his gaze as she passed him some coffee.

"As soft a bed as ever I slept in," he remarked.

"I hope that you slept well," said the girl, civilly.

"Like a child," said Gunn, gravely; "an easy conscience. Eh, Mullet?"

The innkeeper nodded and went on eating. The other, after another remark or two, followed his example, glancing occasionally with warm approval at the beauty of the girl who sat at the head of the table.

"A sweet girl," he remarked, as she withdrew at the end of the meal; "and no mother, I presume?"

"No mother," repeated the other.

Gunn sighed and shook his head.

"A sad case, truly," he murmured. "No mother and such a guardian. Poor soul, if she but knew! Well, we must find her a husband."

He looked down as he spoke, and catching sight of his rusty clothes and broken shoes, clapped his hand to his pocket; and with a glance at his host, sallied out to renew his wardrobe. The innkeeper, with an inscrutable face, watched him down the quay, then with bent head he returned to the house and fell to work on his accounts.

In this work Gunn, returning an hour later, clad from head to foot in new apparel, offered to assist him. Mullett hesitated, but made no demur; neither did he join in the ecstasies which his new partner displayed at the sight of the profits. Gunn put some more gold into his new pockets, and throwing himself back in a chair, called loudly to George to bring him some drink.

In less than a month the intruder was the virtual master of the "Golden Key." Resistance on the part of the legitimate owner became more and more feeble, the slightest objection on his part drawing from the truculent Gunn dark allusions to his past and threats against his future, which for the sake of his daughter he could not ignore. His health began to fail, and Joan watched with perplexed terror the growth of a situation which was in a fair way of becoming unbearable.

The arrogance of Gunn knew no bounds. The maids learned to tremble at his polite grin, or his worse freedom, and the men shrank appalled from his profane wrath. George, after ten years' service, was brutally dismissed, and refusing to accept dismissal from his hands, appealed to his master. The innkeeper confirmed it, and with lack-lustre eyes fenced feebly when his daughter, regardless of Gunn's presence, indignantly appealed to him.

"The man was rude to my friend, my dear," he said dispiritedly

"If he was rude, it was because Mr. Gunn deserved it," said Joan, hotly.

Gunn laughed uproariously.

"Gad, my dear, I like you!" he cried, slapping his leg. "You're a girl of spirit. Now I will make you a fair offer. If you ask for George to stay, stay he shall, as a favour to your sweet self."

The girl trembled.

"Who is master here?" she demanded, turning a full eye on her father.

Mullet laughed uneasily.

"This is business," he said, trying to speak lightly, "and women can't understand it. Gunn is--is valuable to me, and George must go."

"Unless you plead for him, sweet one?" said Gunn.

The girl looked at her father again, but he turned his head away and tapped on the floor with his foot. Then in perplexity, akin to tears, she walked from the room, carefully drawing her dress aside as Gunn held the door for her.

"A fine girl," said Gunn, his thin lips working; "a fine spirit. 'Twill be pleasant to break it; but she does not know who is master here."

"She is young yet," said the other, hurriedly.

"I will soon age her if she looks like that at me again," said Gunn. "By ---, I'll turn out the whole crew into the street, and her with them, an' I wish it. I'll lie in my bed warm o' nights and think of her huddled on a doorstep."

His voice rose and his fists clenched, but he kept his distance and watched the other warily. The innkeeper's face was contorted and his brow grew wet. For one moment something peeped out of his eyes; the next he sat down in his chair again and nervously fingered his chin.

"I have but to speak," said Gunn, regarding him with much satisfaction, "and you will hang, and your money go to the Crown. What will become of her then, think you?"

The other laughed nervously.

"'Twould be stopping the golden eggs," he ventured.

"Don't think too much of that," said Gunn, in a hard voice. "I was never one to be baulked, as you know."

"Come, come. Let us be friends," said Mullet; "the girl is young, and has had her way."

He looked almost pleadingly at the other, and his voice trembled. Gunn drew himself up, and regarding him with a satisfied sneer, quitted the room without a word.

Affairs at the "Golden Key" grew steadily worse and worse. Gunn dominated the place, and his vile personality hung over it like a shadow. Appeals to the innkeeper were in vain; his health was breaking fast, and he moodily declined to interfere. Gunn appointed servants of his own choosing-brazen maids and foul-mouthed men. The old patrons ceased to frequent the "Golden Key," and its bedrooms stood empty. The maids scarcely deigned to take an order from Joan, and the men spoke to her familiarly. In the midst of all this the innkeeper, who had complained once or twice of vertigo, was seized with a fit.

Joan, flying to him for protection against the brutal advances of Gunn, found him lying in a heap behind the door of his small office, and in her fear called loudly for assistance. A little knot of servants collected, and stood regarding him stupidly. One made a brutal jest. Gunn, pressing through the throng, turned the senseless body over with his foot, and cursing vilely, ordered them to carry it upstairs.

Until the surgeon came, Joan, kneeling by the bed, held on to the senseless hand as her only protection against the evil faces of Gunn and his proteges. Gunn himself was taken aback, the innkeeper's death at that time by no means suiting his aims.

The surgeon was a man of few words and fewer attainments, but under his ministrations the innkeeper, after a long interval, rallied. The half- closed eyes opened, and he looked in a dazed fashion at his surroundings. Gunn drove the servants away and questioned the man of medicine. The answers were vague and interspersed with Latin. Freedom from noise and troubles of all kinds was insisted upon and Joan was installed as nurse, with a promise of speedy assistance.

The assistance arrived late in the day in the shape of an elderly woman, whose Spartan treatment of her patients had helped many along the silent road. She commenced her reign by punching the sick man's pillows, and having shaken him into consciousness by this means, gave him a dose of physic, after first tasting it herself from the bottle.

After the first rally the innkeeper began to fail slowly. It was seldom that he understood what was said to him, and pitiful to the beholder to see in his intervals of consciousness his timid anxiety to earn the good- will of the all-powerful Gunn. His strength declined until assistance was needed to turn him in the bed, and his great sinewy hands were forever trembling and fidgeting on the coverlet.

Joan, pale with grief and fear, tended him assiduously. Her stepfather's strength had been a proverb in the town, and many a hasty citizen had felt the strength of his arm. The increasing lawlessness of the house filled her with dismay, and the coarse attentions of Gunn became more persistent than ever. She took her meals in the sick-room, and divided her time between that and her own.

Gunn himself was in a dilemma. With Mullet dead, his power was at an end and his visions of wealth dissipated. He resolved to feather his nest immediately, and interviewed the surgeon. The surgeon was ominously reticent, the nurse cheerfully ghoulish.

"Four days I give him," she said, calmly; "four blessed days, not but what he might slip away at any moment."

Gunn let one day of the four pass, and then, choosing a time when Joan was from the room, entered it for a little quiet conversation. The innkeeper's eyes were open, and, what was more to the purpose, intelligent.

"You're cheating the hangman, after all," snarled Gunn. "I'm off to swear an information."

The other, by a great effort, turned his heavy head and fixed his wistful eyes on him.

"Mercy!" he whispered. "For her sake--give me--a little time!"

"To slip your cable, I suppose," quoth Gunn. "Where's your money? Where's your hoard, you miser?"

Mullet closed his eyes. He opened them again slowly and strove to think, while Gunn watched him narrowly. When he spoke, his utterance was thick and labored.

"Come to-night," he muttered, slowly. "Give me--time--I will make your --your fortune. But the nurse-watches."

"I'll see to her," said Gunn, with a grin. "But tell me now, lest you die first."

"You will--let Joan--have a share?" panted the innkeeper.

"Yes, yes," said Gunn, hastily.

The innkeeper strove to raise himself in the bed, and then fell back again exhausted as Joan's step was heard on the stairs. Gunn gave a savage glance of warning at him, and barring the progress of the girl at the door, attempted to salute her. Joan came in pale and trembling, and falling on her knees by the bedside, took her father's hand in hers and wept over it. The innkeeper gave a faint groan and a shiver ran through his body.

It was nearly an hour after midnight that Nick Gunn, kicking off his shoes, went stealthily out onto the landing. A little light came from the partly open door of the sick-room, but all else was in blackness. He moved along and peered in.

The nurse was siting in a high-backed oak chair by the fire. She had slipped down in the seat, and her untidy head hung on her bosom. A glass stood on the small oak table by her side, and a solitary candle on the high mantel-piece diffused a sickly light. Gunn entered the room, and finding that the sick man was dozing, shook him roughly.

The innkeeper opened his eyes and gazed at him blankly.

"Wake, you fool," said Gunn, shaking him again.

The other roused and muttered something incoherently. Then he stirred slightly.

"The nurse," he whispered.

"She's safe enow," said Gunn. "I've seen to that."

He crossed the room lightly, and standing before the unconscious woman, inspected her closely and raised her in the chair. Her head fell limply over the arm.

"Dead?" inquired Mullet, in a fearful whisper.

"Drugged," said Gunn, shortly. "Now speak up, and be lively."

The innkeeper's eyes again travelled in the direction of the nurse.

"The men," he whispered; "the servants."

"Dead drunk and asleep," said Gunn, biting the words. "The last day would hardly rouse them. Now will you speak, damn you!"

"I must--take care--of Joan," said the father.

Gunn shook his clenched hand at him.

"My money--is--is--" said the other. "Promise me on--your oath--Joan."

"Ay, ay," growled Gunn; "how many more times? I'll marry her, and she shall have what I choose to give her. Speak up, you fool! It's not for you to make terms. Where is it?"

He bent over, but Mullet, exhausted with his efforts, had closed his eyes again, and half turned his head.

"Where is it, damn you?" said Gunn, from between his teeth.

Mullet opened his eyes again, glanced fearfully round the room, and whispered. Gunn, with a stifled oath, bent his ear almost to his mouth, and the next moment his neck was in the grip of the strongest man in Riverstone, and an arm like a bar of iron over his back pinned him down across the bed.

"You dog!" hissed a fierce voice in his ear. "I've got you--Captain Rogers at your service, and now you may tell his name to all you can. Shout it, you spawn of hell. Shout it!"

He rose in bed, and with a sudden movement flung the other over on his back. Gunn's eyes were starting from his head, and he writhed convulsively.

"I thought you were a sharper man, Gunn," said Rogers, still in the same hot whisper, as he relaxed his grip a little; "you are too simple, you hound! When you first threatened me I resolved to kill you. Then you threatened my daughter. I wish that you had nine lives, that I might take them all. Keep still!"

He gave a half-glance over his shoulder at the silent figure of the nurse, and put his weight on the twisting figure on the bed.

"You drugged the hag, good Gunn," he continued. "To-morrow morning,

Gunn, they will find you in your room dead, and if one of the scum you brought into my house be charged with the murder, so much the better. When I am well they will go. I am already feeling a little bit stronger, Gunn, as you see, and in a month I hope to be about again."

He averted his face, and for a time gazed sternly and watchfully at the door. Then he rose slowly to his feet, and taking the dead man in his arms, bore him slowly and carefully to his room, and laid him a huddled heap on the floor. Swiftly and noiselessly he put the dead man's shoes on and turned his pockets inside out, kicked a rug out of place, and put a guinea on the floor. Then he stole cautiously down stairs and set a small door at the back open. A dog barked frantically, and he hurried back to his room. The nurse still slumbered by the fire.

She awoke in the morning shivering with the cold, and being jealous of her reputation, rekindled the fire, and measuring out the dose which the invalid should have taken, threw it away. On these unconscious preparations for an alibi Captain Rogers gazed through half-closed lids, and then turning his grim face to the wall, waited for the inevitable alarm.

DESERTED

Sailormen ain't wot you might call dandyfied as a rule," said the night- watch-man, who had just had a passage of arms with a lighterman and been advised to let somebody else wash him and make a good job of it; "they've got too much sense. They leave dressing up and making eyesores of theirselves to men wot 'ave never smelt salt water; men wot drift up and down the river in lighters and get in everybody's way."

He glanced fiercely at the retreating figure of the lighterman, and, turning a deaf ear to a request for a lock of his hair to patch a favorite doormat with, resumed with much vigor his task of sweeping up the litter.

The most dressy sailorman I ever knew, he continued, as he stood the broom up in a corner and seated himself on a keg, was a young feller named Rupert Brown. His mother gave 'im the name of Rupert while his father was away at sea, and when he came 'ome it was too late to alter it. All that a man could do he did do, and Mrs. Brown 'ad a black eye till 'e went to sea agin. She was a very obstinate woman, though--like most of 'em--and a little over a year arterwards got pore old Brown three months' hard by naming 'er next boy Roderick Alfonso.

Young Rupert was on a barge when I knew 'im fust, but he got tired of always 'aving dirty hands arter a time, and went and enlisted as a soldier. I lost sight of 'im for a while, and then one evening he turned up on furlough and come to see me.

O' course, by this time 'e was tired of soldiering, but wot upset 'im more than anything was always 'aving to be dressed the same and not being able to wear a collar and neck-tie. He said that if it wasn't for the sake of good old England, and the chance o' getting six months, he'd desert. I tried to give 'im good advice, and, if I'd only known 'ow I was to be dragged into it, I'd ha' given 'im a lot more.

As it 'appened he deserted the very next arternoon. He was in the Three Widders at Aldgate, in the saloon bar--which is a place where you get a penn'orth of ale in a glass and pay twopence for it--and, arter being told by the barmaid that she had got one monkey at 'ome, he got into conversation with another man wot was in there.

He was a big man with a black moustache and a red face, and 'is fingers all smothered in di'mond rings. He 'ad got on a gold watch-chain as thick as a rope, and a scarf-pin the size of a large walnut, and he had 'ad a few words with the barmaid on 'is own account. He seemed to take a fancy to Rupert from the fust, and in a few minutes he 'ad given 'im a big cigar out of a sealskin case and ordered 'im a glass of sherry wine.

"Have you ever thought o' going on the stage?" he ses, arter Rupert 'ad told 'im of his dislike for the Army.

"No," ses Rupert, staring.

"You s'prise me," ses the big man; "you're wasting of your life by not doing so."

"But I can't act," ses Rupert.

"Stuff and nonsense!" ses the big man. "Don't tell me. You've got an actor's face. I'm a manager myself, and I know. I don't mind telling you that I refused twenty-three men and forty-eight ladies only yesterday."

"I wonder you don't drop down dead," ses the barmaid, lifting up 'is glass to wipe down the counter.

The manager looked at her, and, arter she 'ad gone to talk to a gentleman in the next bar wot was knocking double knocks on the counter with a pint pot, he whispered to Rupert that she 'ad been one of them.

"She can't act a bit," he ses. "Now, look 'ere; I'm a business man and my time is valuable. I don't know nothing, and I don't want to know nothing; but, if a nice young feller, like yourself, for example, was tired of the Army and wanted to escape, I've got one part left in my company that 'ud suit 'im down to the ground."

"Wot about being reckernized?" ses Rupert.

The manager winked at 'im. "It's the part of a Zulu chief," he ses, in a whisper.

Rupert started. "But I should 'ave to black my face," he ses.

He seemed to take a fancy to Rupert from the fust.

"A little," ses the manager; "but you'd soon get on to better parts--and see wot a fine disguise it is."

He stood 'im two more glasses o' sherry wine, and, arter he' ad drunk 'em, Rupert gave way. The manager patted 'im on the back, and said that if he wasn't earning fifty pounds a week in a year's time he'd eat his 'ead; and the barmaid, wot 'ad come back agin, said it was the best thing he could do with it, and she wondered he 'adn't thought of it afore.

They went out separate, as the manager said it would be better for them not to be seen together, and Rupert, keeping about a dozen yards behind, follered 'im down the Mile End Road. By and by the manager stopped outside a shop-window wot 'ad been boarded up and stuck all over with savages dancing and killing white people and hunting elephants, and, arter turning round and giving Rupert a nod, opened the door with a key and went inside.

"That's all right," he ses, as Rupert follered 'im in. "This is my wife, Mrs. Alfredi," he ses, introducing 'im to a fat, red-'aired lady wot was sitting inside sewing. "She has performed before all the crowned 'eads of Europe. That di'mond brooch she's wearing was a present from the Emperor of Germany, but, being a married man, he asked 'er to keep it quiet."

Rupert shook 'ands with Mrs. Alfredi, and then her 'usband led 'im to a room at the back, where a little lame man was cleaning up things, and told 'im to take his clothes off.

"If they was mine," he ses, squinting at the fire-place, "I should know wot to do with 'em."

Rupert laughed and slapped 'im on the back, and, arter cutting his uniform into pieces, stuffed it into the fireplace and pulled the dampers out. He burnt up 'is boots and socks and everything else, and they all three laughed as though it was the best joke in the world. Then Mr. Alfredi took his coat off and, dipping a piece of rag into a basin of stuff wot George 'ad fetched, did Rupert a lovely brown all over.

"That's the fust coat," he ses. "Now take a stool in front of the fire and let it soak in."

He gave 'im another coat arf an hour arterwards, while George curled his 'air, and when 'e was dressed in bracelets round 'is ankles and wrists, and a leopard-skin over his shoulder, he was as fine a Zulu as you could wish for to see. His lips was

An elderly old party wot would keep jabbing 'im in the ribs with her umbrella.

naturally thick and his nose flat, and even his eyes 'appened to be about the right color.

"He's a fair perfect treat," ses Mr. Alfredi. "Fetch Kumbo in, George."

The little man went out, and came back agin shoving in a fat, stumpy Zulu woman wot began to grin and chatter like a poll-parrot the moment she saw Rupert.

"It's all right," ses Mr. Alfredi; "she's took a fancy to you."

"Is--is she an actress?" ses Rupert.

"One o' the best," ses the manager. "She'll teach you to dance and shy assegais. Pore thing! she buried her 'usband the day afore we come here, but you'll be surprised to see 'ow skittish she can be when she has got over it a bit."

They sat there while Rupert practised--till he started shying the assegais, that is--and then they went out and left 'im with Kumbo. Considering that she 'ad only just buried her 'usband, Rupert found her quite skittish enough, and he couldn't 'elp wondering wot she'd be like when she'd got over her grief a bit more.

The manager and George said he 'ad got on wonderfully, and arter talking it over with Mrs. Alfredi they decided to open that evening, and pore Rupert found out that the shop was the theatre, and all the acting he'd got to do was to dance war-dances and sing in Zulu to people wot had paid a penny a 'ead. He was a bit nervous at fust, for fear anybody should find out that 'e wasn't a real Zulu, because the manager said they'd tear 'im to pieces if they did, and eat 'im arterwards, but arter a time 'is nervousness wore off and he jumped about like a monkey.

They gave performances every arf hour from ha'-past six to ten, and Rupert felt ready to drop. His feet was sore with dancing and his throat ached with singing Zulu, but wot upset 'im more than anything was an elderly old party wot would keep jabbing 'im in the ribs with her umbrella to see whether he could laugh.

They 'ad supper arter they 'ad closed, and then Mr. Alfredi and 'is wife went off, and Rupert and George made up beds for themselves in the shop, while Kumbo 'ad a little place to herself at the back.

He did better than ever next night, and they all said he was improving fast; and Mr. Alfredi told 'im in a whisper that he thought he was better at it than Kumbo. "Not that I should mind 'er knowing much," he ses, "seeing that she's took such a fancy to you."

"Ah, I was going to speak to you about that," ses Rupert. "Forwardness is no name for it; if she don't keep 'erself to 'erself, I shall chuck the whole thing up."

The manager coughed behind his 'and. "And go back to the Army?" he ses. "Well, I should be sorry to lose you, but I won't stand in your way."

Mrs. Alfredi, wot was standing by, stuffed her pocket-'ankercher in 'er mouth, and Rupert began to feel a bit uneasy in his mind.

"If I did," he ses, "you'd get into trouble for 'elping me to desert."

"Desert!" ses Mr. Alfredi. "I don't know anything about your deserting."

"Ho!" ses Rupert. "And wot about my uniform?"

"Uniform?" ses Mr. Alfredi. "Wot uniform? I ain't seen no uniform. Where is it?"

Rupert didn't answer 'im, but arter they 'ad gone 'ome he told George that he 'ad 'ad enough of acting and he should go.

"Where to?" ses George.

"I'll find somewhere," ses Rupert. "I sha'n't starve."

"You might ketch your death o' cold, though," ses George.

Rupert said he didn't mind, and then he shut 'is eyes and pretended to be asleep. His idea was to wait till George was asleep and then pinch 'is clothes; consequently 'is feelings when 'e opened one eye and saw George getting into bed with 'is clothes on won't bear thinking about. He laid awake for hours, and three times that night George, who was a very heavy sleeper, woke up and found Rupert busy tucking him in.

By the end of the week Rupert was getting desperate. He hated being black for one thing, and the more he washed the better color he looked. He didn't mind the black for out o' doors, in case the Army was looking for 'im, but 'aving no clothes he couldn't get out o' doors; and when he said he wouldn't perform unless he got some, Mr. Alfredi dropped 'ints about having 'im took up for a deserter.

"I've 'ad my suspicions of it for some days," he ses, with a wink, "though you did come to me in a nice serge suit and tell me you was an actor. Now, you be a good boy for another week and I'll advance you a couple o' pounds to get some clothes with."

Rupert asked him to let 'im have it then, but 'e wouldn't, and for another week he 'ad to pretend 'e was a Zulu of an evening, and try and persuade Kumbo that he was an English gentleman of a daytime.

He got the money at the end of the week and 'ad to sign a paper to give a month's notice any time he wanted to leave, but he didn't mind that at all, being determined the fust time he got outside the place to run away and ship as a nigger cook if 'e couldn't get the black off.

He made a list o' things out for George to get for 'im, but there seemed to be such a lot for two pounds that Mr. Alfredi shook his 'ead over it; and arter calling 'imself a soft-'arted fool, and saying he'd finish up in the workhouse, he made it three pounds and told George to look sharp.

"He's a very good marketer," he ses, arter George 'ad gone; "he don't mind wot trouble he takes. He'll very likely haggle for hours to get sixpence knocked off the trousers or twopence off the shirt."

It was twelve o'clock in the morning when George went, and at ha'-past four Rupert turned nasty, and said 'e was afraid he was trying to get them for nothing. At five o'clock he said George was a fool, and at ha'-past he said 'e was something I won't repeat.

It was just eleven o'clock, and they 'ad shut up for the night, when the front door opened, and George stood there smiling at 'em and shaking his 'ead.

"Sush a lark," he ses, catching 'old of Mr. Alfredi's arm to steady 'imself. "I gave 'im shlip."

"Wot d'ye mean?" ses the manager, shaking him off. "Gave who the slip? Where's them clothes?"

"Boy's got 'em," ses George, smiling agin and catching hold of Kumbo's arm. "Sush a lark; he's been car-carrying 'em all day--all day. Now I've given 'im the--the shlip, 'stead o'--'stead o' giving 'im fourpence. Take care o' the pensh, an' pouns--"

He let go o' Kumbo's arm, turned round twice, and then sat down 'eavy and fell fast asleep. The manager rushed to the door and looked out, but there was no signs of the boy, and he came back shaking his 'ead, and said that George 'ad been drinking agin.

"Well, wot about my clothes?" ses Rupert, hardly able to speak.

"P'r'aps he didn't buy 'em arter all," ses the manager. "Let's try 'is pockets."

He tried fust, and found some strawberries that George 'ad spoilt by sitting on. Then he told Rupert to have a try, and Rupert found some bits of string, a few buttons, two penny stamps, and twopence ha'penny in coppers.

"Never mind," ses Mr. Alfredi; "I'll go round to the police-station in the morning; p'r'aps the boy 'as taken them there. I'm disapp'inted in George. I shall tell 'im so, too."

He bid Rupert good-night and went off with Mrs. Alfredi; and Rupert, wishful to make the best o' things, decided that he would undress George and go off in 'is clothes. He waited till Kumbo 'ad gone off to bed, and then he started to take George's coat off. He got the two top buttons undone all right, and then George turned over in 'is sleep. It surprised Rupert, but wot surprised 'im more when he rolled George over was to find them two buttons done up agin. Arter it had 'appened three times he see 'ow it was, and he come to the belief that George was no more drunk than wot he was, and that it was all a put-up thing between 'im and Mr. Alfredi.

He went to bed then to think it over, and by the morning he 'ad made up his mind to keep quiet and bide his time, as the saying is. He spoke quite cheerful to Mr. Alfredi, and pretended to believe 'im when he said that he 'ad been to the police-station about the clothes.

Two days arterwards he thought of something; he remembered me. He 'ad found a dirty old envelope on the floor, and with a bit o' lead pencil he wrote me a letter on the back of one o' the bills, telling me all his troubles, and asking me to bring some clothes and rescue 'im. He stuck on one of the stamps he 'ad found in George's pocket, and opening the door just afore going to bed threw it out on the pavement.

The world is full of officious, interfering busy-bodies. I should no more think of posting a letter that didn't belong to me, with an unused stamp on it, than I should think o' flying; but some meddle-some son of a ----a gun posted that letter and I got it.

I was never more surprised in my life. He asked me to be outside the shop next night at ha'-past eleven with any old clothes I could pick up. If I didn't, he said he should 'ang 'imself as the clock struck twelve, and that his ghost would sit on the wharf and keep watch with me every night for the rest o' my life. He said he expected it 'ud have a black face, same as in life.

A wharf is a lonely place of a night; especially our wharf, which is full of dark corners, and, being a silly, good-natured fool, I went. I got a pal off of one of the boats to keep watch for me, and, arter getting some old rags off of another sailorman as owed me arf a dollar, I 'ad a drink and started off for the Mile End Road.

I found the place easy enough. The door was just on the jar, and as I tapped on it with my finger-nails a wild-looking black man, arf naked, opened it and said "H'sh!" and pulled me inside. There was a bit o' candle on the floor, shaded by a box, and a man fast asleep and snoring up in one corner. Rupert dressed like lightning, and he 'ad just put on 'is cap when the door at the back opened and a 'orrid fat black woman came out and began to chatter.

Rupert told her to hush, and she 'ushed, and then he waved 'is hand to 'er to say "good-bye," and afore you could say Jack Robinson she 'ad grabbed up a bit o' dirty blanket, a bundle of assegais, and a spear, and come out arter us.

"Back!" ses Rupert in a whisper, pointing.

Kumbo shook her 'ead, and then he took hold of 'er and tried to shove 'er back, but she wouldn't go. I lent him a 'and, but all wimmen are the same, black or white, and afore I knew where I was she 'ad clawed my cap off and scratched me all down one side of the face.

"Walk fast," ses Rupert.

I started to run, but it was all no good; Kumbo kept up with us easy, and she was so pleased at being out in the open air that she began to dance and play about like a kitten. Instead o' minding their own business people turned and follered us, and quite a crowd collected.

"We shall 'ave the police in a minute," ses Rupert. "Come in 'ere-- quick."

He pointed to a pub up a side street, and went in with Kumbo holding on to his arm. The barman was for sending us out at fust, but such a crowd follered us in that he altered 'is mind. I ordered three pints, and, while I was 'anding Rupert his, Kumbo finished 'ers and began on mine. I tried to explain, but she held on to it like grim death, and in the confusion Rupert slipped out.

He 'adn't been gone five seconds afore she missed 'im, and I never see anybody so upset in all my life. She spilt the beer all down the place where 'er bodice ought to ha' been, and then she dropped the pot and went arter 'im like a hare. I follered in a different way, and when I got round the corner I found she 'ad caught 'im and was holding 'im by the arm.

"Back!" ses Rupert in a whisper, pointing.

O' course, the crowd was round us agin, and to get rid of 'em I did a thing I'd seldom done afore--I called a cab, and we all bundled in and drove off to the wharf, with the spear sticking out o' the window, and most of the assegais sticking into me.

"This is getting serious," ses Rupert.

"Yes," I ses; "and wot 'ave I done to be dragged into it? You must ha' been paying 'er some attention to make 'er carry on like this."

I thought Rupert would ha' bust, and the things he said to the man wot was spending money like water to rescue 'im was disgraceful.

We got to the wharf at last, and I was glad to see that my pal 'ad got tired of night-watching and 'ad gone off, leaving the gate open. Kumbo went in 'anging on to Rupert's arm, and I follered with the spear, which I 'ad held in my 'and while I paid the cabman.

They went into the office, and Rupert and me talked it over while Kumbo kept patting 'is cheek. He was afraid that the manager would track 'im to the wharf, and I was afraid that the guv'nor would find out that I 'ad been neglecting my dooty, for the fust time in my life.

We talked all night pretty near, and then, at ha'-past five, arf an hour afore the 'ands came on, I made up my mind to fetch a cab and drive 'em to my 'ouse. I wanted Rupert to go somewhere else, but 'e said he 'ad got nowhere else to go, and it was the only thing to get 'em off the wharf. I opened the gates at ten minutes to six, and just as the fust man come on and walked down the wharf we slipped in and drove away.

We was all tired and yawning. There's something about the motion of a cab or an omnibus that always makes me feel sleepy, and arter a time I closed my eyes and went off sound. I remember I was dreaming that I 'ad found a bag o' money, when the cab pulled up with a jerk in front of my 'ouse and woke me up. Opposite me sat Kumbo fast asleep, and Rupert 'ad disappeared!

I was dazed for a moment, and afore I could do anything Kumbo woke up and missed Rupert. Wot made matters worse than anything was that my missis was kneeling down in the passage doing 'er door-step, and 'er face, as I got down out o' that cab with Kumbo 'anging on to my arm was something too awful for words. It seemed to rise up slow-like from near the door- step, and to go on rising till I

She stood blocking up the doorway with her 'ands on her 'ips.

thought it 'ud never stop. And every inch it rose it got worse and worse to look at.

She stood blocking up the doorway with her 'ands on her 'ips, while I explained, with Kumbo still 'anging on my arm and a crowd collecting behind, and the more I explained, the more I could see she didn't believe a word of it.

She never 'as believed it. I sent for Mr. Alfredi to come and take Kumbo away, and when I spoke to 'im about Rupert he said I was dreaming, and asked me whether I wasn't ashamed o' myself for carrying off a pore black gal wot 'ad got no father or mother to look arter her. He said that afore my missis, and my character 'as been under a cloud ever since, waiting for Rupert to turn up and clear it away.

The Codes Of Hammurabi And Moses
W. W. Davies

QTY

The discovery of the Hammurabi Code is one of the greatest achievements of archaeology, and is of paramount interest, not only to the student of the Bible, but also to all those interested in ancient history...

Religion   ISBN: *1-59462-338-4*   Pages:132
MSRP $12.95

The Theory of Moral Sentiments
Adam Smith

QTY

This work from 1749. contains original theories of conscience amd moral judgment and it is the foundation for systemof morals.

Philosophy ISBN: *1-59462-777-0*   Pages:536
MSRP $19.95

Jessica's First Prayer
Hesba Stretton

QTY

In a screened and secluded corner of one of the many railway-bridges which span the streets of London there could be seen a few years ago, from five o'clock every morning until half past eight, a tidily set-out coffee-stall, consisting of a trestle and board, upon which stood two large tin cans, with a small fire of charcoal burning under each so as to keep the coffee boiling during the early hours of the morning when the work-people were thronging into the city on their way to their daily toil...

Childrens   ISBN: *1-59462-373-2*   Pages:84
MSRP $9.95

My Life and Work
Henry Ford

QTY

Henry Ford revolutionized the world with his implementation of mass production for the Model T automobile. Gain valuable business insight into his life and work with his own auto-biography... "We have only started on our development of our country we have not as yet, with all our talk of wonderful progress, done more than scratch the surface. The progress has been wonderful enough but..."

Biographies/   ISBN: *1-59462-198-5*   Pages:300
MSRP $21.95

The Art of Cross-Examination
Francis Wellman

QTY

I presume it is the experience of every author, after his first book is published upon an important subject, to be almost overwhelmed with a wealth of ideas and illustrations which could readily have been included in his book, and which to his own mind, at least, seem to make a second edition inevitable. Such certainly was the case with me; and when the first edition had reached its sixth impression in five months, I rejoiced to learn that it seemed to my publishers that the book had met with a sufficiently favorable reception to justify a second and considerably enlarged edition. ..

Pages:412

Reference   ISBN: *1-59462-647-2*   *MSRP $19.95*

On the Duty of Civil Disobedience
Henry David Thoreau

QTY

Thoreau wrote his famous essay, On the Duty of Civil Disobedience, as a protest against an unjust but popular war and the immoral but popular institution of slave-owning. He did more than write—he declined to pay his taxes, and was hauled off to gaol in consequence. Who can say how much this refusal of his hastened the end of the war and of slavery ?

Law   ISBN: *1-59462-747-9*   **Pages:48**

MSRP $7.45

Dream Psychology Psychoanalysis for Beginners
Sigmund Freud

QTY

Sigmund Freud, born Sigismund Schlomo Freud (May 6, 1856 - September 23, 1939), was a Jewish-Austrian neurologist and psychiatrist who co-founded the psychoanalytic school of psychology. Freud is best known for his theories of the unconscious mind, especially involving the mechanism of repression; his redefinition of sexual desire as mobile and directed towards a wide variety of objects; and his therapeutic techniques, especially his understanding of transference in the therapeutic relationship and the presumed value of dreams as sources of insight into unconscious desires.

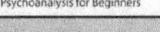

Pages:196

Psychology   ISBN: *1-59462-905-6*   *MSRP $15.45*

The Miracle of Right Thought
Orison Swett Marden

QTY

Believe with all of your heart that you will do what you were made to do. When the mind has once formed the habit of holding cheerful, happy, prosperous pictures, it will not be easy to form the opposite habit. It does not matter how improbable or how far away this realization may see, or how dark the prospects may be, if we visualize them as best we can, as vividly as possible, hold tenaciously to them and vigorously struggle to attain them, they will gradually become actualized, realized in the life. But a desire, a longing without endeavor, a yearning abandoned or held indifferently will vanish without realization.

Pages:360

Self Help   ISBN: *1-59462-644-8*   *MSRP $25.45*

www.bookjungle.com *email: sales@bookjungle.com fax: 630-214-0564 mail: Book Jungle PO Box 2226 Champaign, IL 61825*

QTY

The Rosicrucian Cosmo-Conception Mystic Christianity *by Max Heindel* ISBN: *1-59462-188-8* **$38.95**
The Rosicrucian Cosmo-conception is not dogmatic, neither does it appeal to any other authority than the reason of the student. It is: not controversial, but is: sent forth in the, hope that it may help to clear... New Age/Religion Pages 646

Abandonment To Divine Providence *by Jean-Pierre de Caussade* ISBN: *1-59462-228-0* **$25.95**
"The Rev. Jean Pierre de Caussade was one of the most remarkable spiritual writers of the Society of Jesus in France in the 18th Century. His death took place at Toulouse in 1751. His works have gone through many editions and have been republished... Inspirational/Religion Pages 400

Mental Chemistry *by Charles Haanel* ISBN: *1-59462-192-6* **$23.95**
Mental Chemistry allows the change of material conditions by combining and appropriately utilizing the power of the mind. Much like applied chemistry creates something new and unique out of careful combinations of chemicals the mastery of mental chemistry... New Age Pages 354

The Letters of Robert Browning and Elizabeth Barret Barrett 1845-1846 vol II ISBN: *1-59462-193-4* **$35.95**
by Robert Browning and Elizabeth Barrett Biographies Pages 596

Gleanings In Genesis (volume I) *by Arthur W. Pink* ISBN: *1-59462-130-6* **$27.45**
Appropriately has Genesis been termed "the seed plot of the Bible" for in it we have, in germ form, almost all of the great doctrines which are afterwards fully developed in the books of Scripture which follow... Religion/Inspirational Pages 420

The Master Key *by L. W. de Laurence* ISBN: *1-59462-001-6* **$30.95**
In no branch of human knowledge has there been a more lively increase of the spirit of research during the past few years than in the study of Psychology, Concentration and Mental Discipline. The requests for authentic lessons in Thought Control, Mental Discipline and... New Age/Business Pages 422

The Lesser Key Of Solomon Goetia *by L. W. de Laurence* ISBN: *1-59462-092-X* **$9.95**
This translation of the first book of the "Lernegton" which is now for the first time made accessible to students of Talismanic Magic was done, after careful collation and edition, from numerous Ancient Manuscripts in Hebrew, Latin, and French... New Age/Occult Pages 92

Rubaiyat Of Omar Khayyam *by Edward Fitzgerald* ISBN:*1-59462-332-5* **$13.95**
Edward Fitzgerald, whom the world has already learned, in spite of his own efforts to remain within the shadow of anonymity, to look upon as one of the rarest poets of the century, was born at Bredfield, in Suffolk, on the 31st of March, 1809. He was the third son of John Purcell... Music Pages 172

Ancient Law *by Henry Maine* ISBN: *1-59462-128-4* **$29.95**
The chief object of the following pages is to indicate some of the earliest ideas of mankind, as they are reflected in Ancient Law, and to point out the relation of those ideas to modern thought. Religiom/History Pages 452

Far-Away Stories *by William J. Locke* ISBN: *1-59462-129-2* **$19.45**
"Good wine needs no bush, but a collection of mixed vintages does. And this book is just such a collection. Some of the stories I do not want to remain buried for ever in the museum files of dead magazine-numbers an author's not unpardonable vanity..." Fiction Pages 272

Life of David Crockett *by David Crockett* ISBN: *1-59462-250-7* **$27.45**
"Colonel David Crockett was one of the most remarkable men of the times in which he lived. Born in humble life, but gifted with a strong will, an indomitable courage, and unremitting perseverance... Biographies/New Age Pages 424

Lip-Reading *by Edward Nitchie* ISBN: *1-59462-206-X* **$25.95**
Edward B. Nitchie, founder of the New York School for the Hard of Hearing, now the Nitchie School of Lip-Reading, Inc, wrote "LIP-READING Principles and Practice". The development and perfecting of this meritorious work on lip-reading was an undertaking... How-to Pages 400

A Handbook of Suggestive Therapeutics, Applied Hypnotism, Psychic Science ISBN: *1-59462-214-0* **$24.95**
by Henry Munro Health/New Age/Health/Self-help Pages 376

A Doll's House: and Two Other Plays *by Henrik Ibsen* ISBN: *1-59462-112-8* **$19.95**
Henrik Ibsen created this classic when in revolutionary 1848 Rome. Introducing some striking concepts in playwriting for the realist genre, this play has been studied the world over. Fiction/Classics/Plays 308

The Light of Asia *by sir Edwin Arnold* ISBN: *1-59462-204-3* **$13.95**
In this poetic masterpiece, Edwin Arnold describes the life and teachings of Buddha. The man who was to become known as Buddha to the world was born as Prince Gautama of India but he rejected the worldly riches and abandoned the reigns of power when... Religion/History/Biographies Pages 170

The Complete Works of Guy de Maupassant *by Guy de Maupassant* ISBN: *1-59462-157-8* **$16.95**
"For days and days, nights and nights, I had dreamed of that first kiss which was to consecrate our engagement, and I knew not on what spot I should put my lips..." Fiction/Classics Pages 240

The Art of Cross-Examination *by Francis L. Wellman* ISBN: *1-59462-309-0* **$26.95**
Written by a renowned trial lawyer, Wellman imparts his experience and uses case studies to explain how to use psychology to extract desired information through questioning. How-to/Science/Reference Pages 408

Answered or Unanswered? *by Louisa Vaughan* ISBN: *1-59462-248-5* **$10.95**
Miracles of Faith in China Religion Pages 112

The Edinburgh Lectures on Mental Science (1909) *by Thomas* ISBN: *1-59462-008-3* **$11.95**
This book contains the substance of a course of lectures recently given by the writer in the Queen Street Hail, Edinburgh. Its purpose is to indicate the Natural Principles governing the relation between Mental Action and Material Conditions... New Age/Psychology Pages 148

Ayesha *by H. Rider Haggard* ISBN: *1-59462-301-5* **$24.95**
Verily and indeed it is the unexpected that happens! Probably if there was one person upon the earth from whom the Editor of this, and of a certain previous history, did not expect to hear again... Classics Pages 380

Ayala's Angel *by Anthony Trollope* ISBN: *1-59462-352-X* **$29.95**
The two girls were both pretty, but Lucy who was twenty-one who supposed to be simple and comparatively unattractive, whereas Ayala was credited, as her Bombwhat romantic name might show, with poetic charm and a taste for romance. Ayala when her father died was nineteen... Fiction Pages 484

The American Commonwealth *by James Bryce* ISBN: *1-59462-286-8* **$34.45**
An interpretation of American democratic political theory. It examines political mechanics and society from the perspective of Scotsman James Bryce Politics Pages 572

Stories of the Pilgrims *by Margaret P. Pumphrey* ISBN: *1-59462-116-0* **$17.95**
This book explores pilgrims religious oppression in England as well as their escape to Holland and eventual crossing to America on the Mayflower, and their early days in New England... History Pages 268

QTY

The Fasting Cure *by Sinclair Upton*   ISBN: *1-59462-222-1* **$13.95**

In the Cosmopolitan Magazine for May, 1910, and in the Contemporary Review (London) for April, 1910, I published an article dealing with my experi-
ences in fasting. I have written a great many magazine articles, but never one which attracted so much attention... New Age/Self Help/Health Pages 164

Hebrew Astrology *by Sepharial*   ISBN: *1-59462-308-2* **$13.45**

In these days of advanced thinking it is a matter of common observation that we have left many of the old landmarks behind and that we are now pressing
forward to greater heights and to a wider horizon than that which represented the mind-content of our progenitors...   Astrology Pages 144

Thought Vibration or The Law of Attraction in the Thought World   ISBN: *1-59462-127-6* **$12.95**

by William Walker Atkinson   *Psychology/Religion Pages 144*

Optimism *by Helen Keller*   ISBN: *1-59462-108-X* **$15.95**

Helen Keller was blind, deaf, and mute since 19 months old, yet famously learned how to overcome these handicaps, communicate with the world, and
spread her lectures promoting optimism. An inspiring read for everyone...   Biographies/Inspirational Pages 84

Sara Crewe *by Frances Burnett*   ISBN: *1-59462-360-0*   **$9.45**

In the first place, Miss Minchin lived in London. Her home was a large, dull, tall one, in a large, dull square, where all the houses were alike, and all the
sparrows were alike, and where all the door-knockers made the same heavy sound...   Childrens/Classic Pages 88

The Autobiography of Benjamin Franklin *by Benjamin Franklin*   ISBN: *1-59462-135-7* **$24.95**

The Autobiography of Benjamin Franklin has probably been more extensively read than any other American historical work, and no other book of its kind
has had such ups and downs of fortune. Franklin lived for many years in England, where he was agent...   Biographies/History Pages 332

Name	
Email	
Telephone	
Address	
City, State ZIP	

☐ **Credit Card**   ☐ **Check / Money Order**

Credit Card Number	
Expiration Date	
Signature	

Please Mail to: Book Jungle
                  PO Box 2226
                  Champaign, IL 61825
or Fax to: 630-214-0564

ORDERING INFORMATION

web*: www.bookjungle.com*
email*: sales@bookjungle.com*
fax*: 630-214-0564*
mail*: Book Jungle PO Box 2226 Champaign, IL 61825*
or PayPal *to sales@bookjungle.com*

Please contact us for bulk discounts

DIRECT-ORDER TERMS

20% Discount if You Order
Two or More Books
Free Domestic Shipping!
Accepted: Master Card, Visa,
Discover, American Express